LUCID REALITY

Serial One: Omnipresence

LINKS & SOCIAL MEDIA

If you enjoyed the book, the best thing you can do for an indie author like myself is leave a review from where you purchased the book and any other social media outlets you enjoy. Let others know what you think, including the author. Your reviews are appreciated.

For news on all creative projects of M.D. Boncher, you can find updates, communication and news at Resonant Point:

www.thedreamnebula.com

www.resonantmedia.art

BIBLIOGRAPHY

Wild Adventure Sci-Fi

Tales From the Dream Nebula

01. Dreams Within Dreams

02. Lucid Reality

03. The Waking Nightmares

Dark Christian Fantasy

Akiniwazisaga

A Light Rises in a Dark World

The Inheritance Thieves

Into The High Places

TABLE OF CONTENTS

TALES from the
DREAM NEBULA
02

1.

The "Cloud9 Port-O'-Call" was a cheis-hole rock of heat-blasted dust, just inside a dry band of the Dream's atmosphere. Nothing more than a way-point for long-haul sky truckers. Here they could stop for maintenance, supplies and to socialize in person.

Mother decided their virtual instance was not much better. It dripped with a gritty grindhouse "cinéma vérité" vibe she found tacky. Rather than polishing off the rough edges, it showcased them, as if every spot of rust and dent was a point of pride. It was like she was in some perverse southwestern horror movie.

Winston should have checked in by now. This wasn't like him. No, wait, she reconsidered. It was completely like him.

He was probably simmed out and she wouldn't hear anything for maybe an hour or two. Perhaps a comm would wake him up. There was a good chance he was close enough to livestream. She made a quick try, but no one answered. A check for his nav beacon and found it was functional, meaning there wasn't any damage to block her, and they were in range. The *Sierra Madre* was in autistic mode, which blocked or ignored all outside signals. That wasn't typical.

She would have to wait. That did not sweeten her spirit.

~   ~   ~

The *Sierra Madre* coasted along at a dead-slow pace. For the last few hours, Billy Joe busied himself with minor repairs on one of their container exteriors. He had given up doing repairs inside. It was too frustrating with all the refugees. They were always in the way.

A patient tried to eat his utility sand skirt. They claimed it looked like "smoked maple syrup with sugar crystal crumbly bits."

Then there was the constant flood of questions from passengers for whom he had no answer.

Yes, we are safe.

Yes, we would unload soon.

Don't touch that!

No. I don't know what time dinner is.

How should I know if that's infected? See a nurse.

No. I don't want to play holocards.

Stop grabbing my nanosand. I don't grab your hair!

He estimated the refugees had enough water, emergency rations, and medical supplies to last them a day or two. Still, Billy Joe sure hoped they could offload these people before things got ugly. Bionts got dangerous when deprived of the essentials of life and comfort. Visualizing the possible food riot gave Billy Joe a little shudder.

He finished grinding smooth the last remnants of a new spot weld's rough edges. Now the lock latched as intended. Satisfied, he went forward to the cab. The airlock closed behind him, making a sigh that echoed his frustration.

While putting his tools away, he heard a computer alert bleeping. He slid over to see they were an hour out of their destination. The comm suite next to it showed a pending message from Mother. He tapped it open and read she was now in livecomm range. That was good enough for him. Time to wake Hoss.

Winston must have gotten eight hours of sleep, according to Billy Joe's internal clock. The indu slid over to the sleeper door and gave it a heavy rap.

"Yo, Hoss!" he yelled. "Time to get yo'self up!"

No answer.

"Hoss!" he shouted again. This time he banged the door a lot harder.

There was a muffled sound of movement, but again no answer.

"Come on, son, Mother's on the horn and she wants ta talk."

Billy Joe hoped Winston had not locked himself in his Levitown instance again. He switched his focus over to the *Sierra Madre's* virtual interface and dove into the server. There he called up Winston's private node and tried to enter.

An error message popped up. His attempt to access Winston's home instance was rebuffed. Did the launcher crash? Miss Holly had done an awful lot of damage to the server that was beyond his repair skills.

Billy Joe made a second attempt. After a long lag, the instance accepted his login. Irritated, he ran the repair tool and took a diagnostic snapshot of the program. The instance launcher wasn't crashed but was stuck. The loading montage was caught in a loop. Had the program gone corrupt?

He went into the bio-rhythmic data log to see what went wrong. Something wasn't right. This should be easy to open, but the program seemed frozen. A power flux could have done it but they hadn't suffered any disruptions. Winston would have rebooted his software within seconds if this was the case. Otherwise, it would have kicked him out of the launcher as a safety feature.

Billy Joe opened the only file he could, the error log. The same message ran every second for tens of thousands of seconds.

~   ~   ~

```
<<ERROR: #1279374.34VIT>>
<!Concussion detected!>
<!Simulation can not connect!>
<Reason: Medical obstruction to neural
induction relays>
<Reason: Transmitters misaligned/out of
safe tolerance parameters>
<!*SYNAPSE BURN DETECTED*!>
<!*SEEK IMMEDIATE MEDICAL ASSISTANCE*!>
```

~   ~   ~

Billy Joe snapped back to the real world and slammed open the sleeper door. Winston was half-rolled over on his side, not flat on his back like how he normally slept. Like a snake, a glossy black arm thrust a pistol out from under Winston's armpit and fired twice.

The low-aimed rounds, intended to blow an intruder's legs off, struck Billy Joe's utility skirt. Splatters of gooey sand sprayed all over the sleeper and cab, then quickly flowed back to reintegrate with him.

"Nahq it all!" he shouted and surged his nanosand out to seize his attacker.

Billy Joe's arms transformed into tendrils and he slithered them around Winston's unconscious body. Holly screamed more in surprise than terror as they wrapped about her like enraged pythons. He jerked her out from behind Winston's unconscious body and slammed her into the ceiling with a loud bang. Dazed, she dropped her pistol.

"You lying, backstabbing, abominable little...! I should crush you right now! What did you do to him, you whore!" Billy Joe's arms wound tighter around her limbs like a hungry octopus wrapping up a crab.

Holly could only grunt and wheeze with her rib cage and abdomen compressing in his industrial-strength coils. "I... I didn't mean... t... to hurt you, Billy Joe."

"And that's why y'shot me? By mistake? But hurtin' Hoss, that was on purpose?" His auto-tuned growl fuzzed with a hot static buzz.

"Wanted... to p- hkkk... prove- who's boss. Didn't mean... t' knoooohhhhhh...hck- knock him out," Holly pleaded.

Her eyes shimmered with pretty tears of agony. Billy Joe was immune to her begging and manipulative beauty. She squirmed but even her enhanced strength was insignificant compared to his own. He could move ten-ton pallets. Nothing she could do could compare to that. A few more pascals of pressure and he would pulp her.

Warnings from his morality governors began flashing red in his mind's eye as he inched up to her fatal limits. A little more and his behavioral safety interlocks would shut him down.

With a sigh, her grimace went slack with relief. Billy Joe realized her pain editors kicked in. The torment was no longer a factor for her.

"That ain't helpin' your situation none, Miss Holly," he said, then drew her face close to his. "Besides, I'm of good mind to let you float home." His threat was a soft rumble.

Holly's eyes shot wide open. "No, ple-hheeeeee..ase! I c'n- hkk… hhhuuu...make this right," she squealed pitifully, using the teaspoon of breath she was still able to draw.

Billy Joe considered her claim. Little red warnings still pulsed in his processor. A timer was now ticking down toward forced shutdown if he did not abort.

He looked at Winston, who gurgled a little in his catatonic state. His glazed eyes twitched in random directions. That synapse burn looked more serious than he knew how to deal with.

"All right. I may need yer help in landing us. So I'll let you live. But if'n you cross me, I'll chuck you overboard faster'n you could slap a horsefly." Billy Joe drove his point home with a final sharp squeeze, like a boa constrictor's heart-stopping crush. Slowly, he put her down. The red warnings from his morality governors went back to green.

A few plates in Holly's armor, deformed by Billy Joe's squeeze, sprung back into shape with hollow pops. Now that her lungs could fully expand again, she noisily sucked in air.

Billy Joe watched her as she sprawled against the wall next to Winston's body. Her hands drifted to her empty holsters.

"How stupid do y'think I am?" Billy Joe said.

Holly gave him a confused look.

Billy Joe drew her pistols and magazines out from his utility skirt. They were encapsulated in a pair of pseudopods. "You kin have these back when I think yer trustworthy again or off my airship."

"Force of habit. I just reacted," she groaned.

"I don't care," Billy Joe's words dripped with venom. The pseudopods melted back into his lower half, hiding the weapons again.

"You made your point. I'll play it straight," she said, sitting up.

"How you gonna make things right? Hoss needs medical help, and not from those brain butchers in back," Billy Joe demanded.

"Brain butchers?" Holly coughed.

"Yeah, those doctors that run the nut hut we just rescued? Remember?" Billy Joe asked.

"And you don't trust 'em. All right. I get that," Holly said with a weak nod.

"So how you gonna fix this?" Billy Joe loomed over the wired assassin.

"I dunno. I'm not qualified to deal with synapse burn from a cheap induction rig," she snapped petulantly. She didn't dare meet his glowering eyes. Billy Joe realized she'd been running her mouth to stay alive. The urge to chuck her off the *Sierra Madre* quickly returned.

"It wasn't a cheap inductor that caused this!" Billy Joe snapped. "You gave him a concussion! Tha's what did it!"

Holly's face drained of color, her lips and eyes paling to near white.

"You didn't know that?" Billy Joe realized, surprised at her reaction.

"No," she whispered hoarsely. "I was tired and upset. I thought I just rung his bell and he'd sleep it off, so I put his rig on him because that's what he always seemed to do. If... if I knew he had a concussion... and I didn't... I'd have never put it on him."

"So do you actually know how to get him back?" Billy Joe demanded, sliding in close, looming over her hunched figure.

"Not really. The people who would know are the ones you don't want to involved with this. They have the equipment and the training," Holly admitted.

"Then we gotta get some other ideas on what to do," Billy Joe concluded and went back to the cab. "Come on. You're gonna have to explain to Mother what you done, Miss Holly."

2

Billy Joe commed and Mother linked to the ship's cab holo projector.

"It's about time. Why have you been in autistic mode?" she grumped, then paused at what she saw.

Winston was not in the pilot seat. Instead, a stunning blue-haired woman in glossy black smartex and pandifico body armor sat there. Billy Joe towered over the woman with a menacing air.

"What is this? Some kind of sick joke? Why is a sex doll in Winston's seat?" Mother snapped, looking around the cab for him. "Winston? Explain yourself."

"I'm not a sex doll!" Holly pouted.

"Prostitute then," Mother said, dismissing her.

"Hey!" Holly protested.

Mother ignored her. "Winston! Where's Winston? What is going on?"

"Mother," Billy Joe said, "We have a serious problem."

"How serious?" Mother's skepticism was thick.

"Life and death," Billy Joe said.

"Winston's? Yours?" Mother's eyes narrowed.

"Yeah. Lemme shoot you a synopsis of our situation," Billy Joe said and launched the data packet to Mother.

"Received," she replied.

A few seconds later, her stern face softened. She wrung her hands while formulating a plan of action. Then just as quickly, her trademark grimace snapped back.

"Here is what I need you to do: Get Winston up and walking. He's going to be a bit of a zombie, but right now he needs to get some real-world stimulation to his brain. Moving around and experiencing tactile sensations will help. Nothing simulated. Not even video screens, just to be safe."

"Yes, ma'am," Billy Joe agreed. All screens and holograms save for the barest essentials of gauges winked out at the mechoid's remote command.

"And make the party girl do it. Xiao knows she's stimulating enough," Mother sniped.

"I'm not-"

"I don't care what you are!" Mother shouted as the cab audio speakers cranked up to max volume.

Mother's fury pounded Holly down into the pilot's seat, her whole face pinched in at the sonic blast.

"You caused this predicament and I'm volun-telling you, you're going to get him out of it! Understood?" Mother ordered.

Holly's eyes slowly peeled open. Her gobsmacked, wide-eyed expression told Mother she got the point.

"What about the containers and those people?" Billy Joe asked.

"Worry about the containers later, and say nothing to those people for now. This is not a

conversation for even an encrypted comm."
Mother gave a deep sigh. "Land on Cloud9 and
put yourself in a deep part of the trailer lot by
long-term storage far away from everything. I'll
pay the parking fee out of a different account.
Then you stay put till I come get you."

"Come get us?" Holly said, surprised.

"When you land on Cloud9, I will load up in a
rental mechbody and come and get you so we
can talk safely."

"Umm..." Holly muttered.

"What 'umm'? Explain yourself!" Mother
blasted.

"We're not going there," Holly said.

"What?" Billy Joe and Mother shouted in
unison.

"I kinda took the initiative and set our course
to Nova Tortuga," Holly wheedled. She looked like
a little girl discovering her initiative had not been
very helpful.

"Oh, that's just it, Dolly!" Mother raged. "Yet
another complication."

"Holly," she sniped back.

"You worry about keeping Winston stimulated, Dolly, but keep it in your... suit." Mother gestured a rebuke at Holly. "Behnging biomes. I don't want to have to untangle even more psychological damage on top of what's already done. It's going to be rough enough as it is," Mother said dismissively.

"I'm not a sex worker!" Holly pouted again.

"No? Then don't wear the uniform!" The ice-cold arch of her eyebrow added to Mother's insult. She went back to calculating their options. "Let me see, let me see," she mulled, her hologram walking around the cab.

"All right, I'll come to you," she declared, coming to an abrupt stop. She spun around her heel. "Billy Joe?"

"Yes, 'um?" he stuttered, blinking in surprise.

"Fetch whoever is in charge of that asylum to the cab and we will have a talk. But first, clear some server space. Mother's coming for a visit." She cut off the comm leaving Billy Joe and a stunned Holly alone.

"How the purg am I supposed to keep him stimulated?" Holly whined.

"Get him up and walk him around the cab a few hundred times. And talk to him," Billy Joe suggested.

"What should I say?" she asked.

"I don't know and really don't care. Recite poetry, tell him dirty limericks. Recite nursery rhymes. Tell 'im your business plan for a network marketing scheme. Anything. Sing if you can or must. It don't matter, just don't turn on that behnging limbic manipulator. That's part of what got us into this mess," he said.

The worry and pain over Winston's predicament was too much for Billy Joe's limited processing. He gave a strange sigh as he shut down his emotion chip to free up processor power consumed by worry.

"What are you going to do?" Holly demanded as she walked to the sleeper to get Winston up and moving.

"What Mother asked. I'm goin' back to fetch the mench in charge of that insane asylum, and we're gonna have a talk," he answered.

3..

Holly had run out of things to say. She finished a laundry list of her thoughts and moved on to the latest imperial outer court gossip. The diabolic schemes of court social climbers looking to steal crumbs of power were almost too numerous to count. If Winston was aware of any of this, it would have been quite an education.

She helped him climb the keel airlock ladder for what seemed to be the hundredth time, then paused. Something felt off. She considered Winston's movements.

"You're improving!" she said in astonishment. He was carrying most of his weight now. "Thank Xiao," she breathed.

She still had to protect him from falling, but he was almost free-standing now. Carefully, she brought him back into the cab and walked

Winston around the trio of crew seats a few more times.

The service airlock hissed open, and a sour-faced dark-skinned man came in.

"Took you long enough, Billy Joe. This must be Dr. O'Chaudry," Holly said. The man had a fleshy round face that radiated disapproval. Behind him followed Dr. Junker. Billy Joe brought up the rear of the procession.

"Where is this sentient who summoned me?" Dr. O'Chaudry sniffed.

"I paged Mother. She'll join us any second now," Billy Joe said.

Dr. Junker stared at Holly who steadied Winston's listing frame. She gave a blink of surprise, unsure of what was going on.

"Are you our pilot?" he demanded of Winston. His eyebrows furrowed more. "This mench has synapse burn."

"Yeah, he's got brainburn. Came from an induction rig after he got a concussion," Holly said.

Dr. Junker hustled over and did a quick medical assessment of Winston. O'Chaudry watched silently.

"How did he get a concussion? We didn't experience any turbulence that I know of," Dr. Junker demanded.

"There was an, ahem… issue. I had to subdue him," Holly said.

"'Cause y'all provoked him," Billy Joe added. Holly glared back. "I'm not gonna let you whitewash what you did, Miss Holly. No ma'am."

Dr. O'Chaudry made a disgusted sound at the revelation.

Billy Joe got close to the doctor and stuck a fat nanosand finger in his face. "Don't you take that tone, Doctor Chaudry. He's our pilot and a nahq good one too. Saved your bacon," Billy Joe defended.

"That's O'Chaudry." The administrator's tone was caustic.

Billy Joe rolled his eyes, confirming to Holly his emotional subroutines were on again.

"What have you been doing to treat Winston?" Dr. Junker asked.

"Got him up and walking. Talking to him, giving real-world stimulation. No simulation. It's the only solution we have," Holly said.

Doctor Junker pursed her lips, dissatisfied at the course of treatment. Holly gave her a challenging, hostile squint back. The two women held each other's gaze. Holly ended the brief standoff with a quick shrug and a sniff.

"Fine. If nobody minds, I'm gonna put our boy down for a bit. He's getting heavy," she announced. With a semi-careless push, she flopped Winston into the pilot's seat.

Dr. O'Chaudry puffed himself up and stepped to Billy Joe. "Let's get this over with. Where are we and where are we going? Thirteen hours of riding in cattle cars have not been an enjoyable experience. My patients have specific needs that must be met soon." He crossed his arms and glared at the indu.

"Nobody's doin' nothing until Mother arrives," Billy Joe shot back, metaphorically putting his foot down. "Till she comms, I'm the highest-ranking officer of this tug, and we sit tight till that happens."

Dr. O'Chaudry thrust his finger in the loadmaster's face. "Look here, Mechster Billy Joe-"

"Shut the behng up," Holly snapped, cutting the administrator off. "There are things we need to find out first. Mother is the only one we trust to have trustworthy intel needed to make smart decisions on what we do next. We know what kind of outfit you're running. Or rather you were running." Holly's goosing of the past tense brought a smile out from Dr. Junker.

"I assure you," O'Chaudry jabbed an accusing finger at Doctor Junker, "anything she might have told you is a mendacious lie! We are an honest and legitimate business. Our credentials and standing in local and imperial law are excellent," he huffed.

"Save it for your stockholders! I've seen what you do!" Dr. Junker fired back.

A chime from the pilot's suite interrupted the shouting. Mother's download was complete.

The holoprojector hummed and Mother's hologram flickered to life at the nose of the cab. A streak of white hair swept through her blonde hair which was fashioned into a tight bun. She wore a conservative pale jade-colored business suit designed for high-stakes arbitrage.

"Billy Joe, that server is a mess! Files everywhere and so much wasted space. I'm surprised you can fly this thing with all those corrupted sectors. You need to get that cleaned up and optimized," Mother griped.

"Yes'um," Billy Joe jeered. "I'll just play data janilor on top of all my other duties."

"Don't sass me, Bubby," she warned with a sharp stab of her finger. "We've got enough trouble without you cracking wise."

"Beg y'er pardon, Ma'am." Billy Joe mumbled.

"Is this everyone here who needs to be? I don't want to repeat our little discussion."

"A quick question, Ma'am," Billy Joe hazarded.

"What now?" She crossed her arms.

"Why are you downloaded here? Why not comm?"

"What we're about to discuss is so sensitive we cannot risk anyone listening in on our data link. The ears and eyes of the empire are sweeping this sector, and thanks to Winston choosing this moment to be a hero, things got complicated." Mother looked about the cab, searching for something. Her eyes locked onto the pilot's chair holo instrumentation. The screens began flickering through a thousand different collections of data.

"What are you looking for?" Dr. O'Chaudry demanded. "I have many pressing matters I must get back to."

"Save that uppity tone for your servants, staff, or whatever little ball of brainwashed fluff you cheat on your wife with, Doctor. You are in no position to demand anything from me." Mother didn't bother to look at O'Chaudry as she excoriated him.

"Coming here sure brought out the fire in her!" Holly muttered to Billy Joe.

"You ain't seen nothin' yet," Billy Joe whispered back.

"We need to make sure nobody's listening in. Thus I'm checking for surveillance and tightening the autistic mode," Mother elaborated. The screens stopped scrolling and went back to their normal display.

"What is going on?" Dr. Junker asked.

"All right, we're as isolated as I can make us. Down to business," Mother declared, satisfied. "First let's deal with your interests," she addressed Dr. O'Chaudry.

"Finally," he groused.

"I've been doing a little background check on you and your firm," she said.

O'Chaudry was smooth as ghee. "We've done nothing wrong."

"Are you confident enough that your conduct will withstand prosecutorial scrutiny from the Kingdom of Gaxsony? They do have control over some of this cluster if the current charts are correct."

"Preposterous!" Dr. O'Chaudry exploded.

"One thing I've learned in my time in transportation is that most people forget to cover their logistical tracks. Mind you, I don't have any hard evidence yet. I'm sure that If I turned over what I do have to a forensic dataoid, they'd find cheis soon enough." Mother threatened.

Dr. O'Chaudry breathed a deep sigh. "So it's blackmail?" he said, rubbing his cheek, his gloomy expression revealing his discontent with the situation he found himself in.

Mother tapped a finger on her chin and looked at the ceiling, thinking. Holly smirked at her mockery. It was clear that the cagey dataoid had O'Chaudry right where she wanted him.

"Only by the broadest definition of the term. Consider this your shock collar to remind you who's in charge if you should give me too much grief. Now, be a good boy, and we'll both be out of each other's hair soon. Then you can remember how you're not a statistic in a mass casualty event, and we can both forget the other exists. Take heart that we currently have no interest in you and your corporation. That means you get to return fairly quickly to whatever shady business you're in. How's that sound for a deal?"

"Better than what I expected," he said, shrugging.

"Good. But if you spam me off, there will be a bill in your inbox that will be very hard to explain to your investors," Mother warned.

"All right. Where are we parting ways?" Dr. O'Chaudry asked.

"Nova Tortuga," Mother said.

One of O'Chaudry's eyes started to twitch with that name, and a furtive flick of the eyes went towards Doctor Junker.

"Nova Tortuga," he muttered, the corners of his mouth drawing tight with the name.

"All nations, tribes and imperial forces in this sector are on high alert thanks to the Blaugarten Black Void. First responders and security are filling this layer fast. I'm certain they are thoroughly inspecting all airships, skytrains, planes and dirigibles in this sector. None of us want such intense scrutiny pointed our way. I, for one, do not wish to find ourselves in Xiao's tender mercies. Do you?"

"Nova Tortuga? No. Unacceptable," Dr. O'Chaudry refused. "We have several facilities in the area that would allow you to drop us off," He counter-offered.

"Not a chance. You are under the mistaken impression this is a negotiation." Mother's voice dripped with icy venom. "None of us will risk institutionalization or having our code overwritten. Nova Tortuga is neutral ground for everyone."

Dr. O'Chaudry grimaced at Mother's accusation, giving Holly a little stab of glee. He looked at Doctor Junker trying to glean a tell from her body language. The woman radiated anger like a heat lamp at his suggestion of another Bonavitae facility.

"Don't look so surprised. You're not as cunning as you think," Mother said. "Once we land there, you can contact your corporate masters. They can come get you or provide funds with which you can return home. Whatever is most convenient."

Silence stretched out between the quartet as they considered the ultimatum. From the pilot's chair, Winston made a nonsensical gurgle. The soft rattling of light turbulence on the *Sierra Madre* was the only indicator of time's passing.

"It seems I have little choice but to agree," Dr. O'Chaudry said, arms open wide.

"I need you to keep your patients under control till we can negotiate a quiet offload. We can't just open the doors on the Nova Tortuga docks and let you fend for yourself. That level of chaos will not do. It's best we conduct this professionally and smoothly for your sake as well as ours," Mother proposed. "Will you do this?"

"We can, but how are we going to provide the medical, food, and sewage needs for these people? It's getting nasty back there."

"We'll organize something if we must," Mother said. "We have some supplies to share with essential personnel and I doubt very highly you lack enough emergency nanofabs to handle your needs. No one's going to die of dehydration or starvation in a day or so. If you didn't bring enough medications for at least a week, I'd be shocked. Use their waste as nanofab feedstock if you must. At least it will keep it cleaner. To ease these difficult times for the more delicate patients, I suggest sedation. That will shield them from the potential chaos and make your lives easier."

Holly could not help but be impressed with Mother's acumen. She boxed the administrator in but was gracious enough to let him save face.

Dr. O'Chaudry chewed his lips, considering the solution. "I'll go inform my staff," he agreed.

"Billy Joe?" Mother asked. "Escort him back. Dr. Junker, please stay a bit longer. I have some bones to pick with you."

41.

Once Billy Joe and Doctor O'Chaudry were in the first container Mother gave a cool smile to Dr. Junker and began.

"And what kind of doctor are you?" Mother asked, arching an eyebrow.

"I hold several doctorates. I assisted my husband in his work," she answered, stiffening at the sudden question.

"What sort of work?" Mother pressed.

"He was a scientist and engineer. My training involved downloads under his supervision. He implanted my doctorates in nano-engineering, cybernetics and bio-engineering. I have degrees in civil, electrical and aerospace engineering, mechanical chemistry, organic chemistry, biology plus genetic medicine."

Holly gave an impressed moue.

"Rare for a biologic to take on such a heavy set of downloads. Did you have any retention loss?" Mother asked.

"Not much. I have had several refreshers to update and reinforce my knowledge," Dr. Junker said. "He put my skills to use in his lab."

"Who did he work for?" Mother asked.

"No one. He was an independent scientist," the widow gave a sharp exhale and matched the intensity of Mother's gaze. "His estate and title allowed him that much."

"Title?" Holly perked up.

"My husband was the Baron Stephon Junker. Heir of the Commonwealth of Puala'Lolo in the Lumina Reaches," Dr. Junker stated. "Absentee member of the Imperial Court of the Seventh Array. One of the Outer Courts of Xiao, and under heavy disfavor with his peers."

Mother nodded while she did a fast scan of public databases. "A collection of skylands and.. hmm! A small planetoid that borders the far up-northern edges of the outer kingdoms... near Nova Tortuga. How convenient," Mother smirked.

"Very. We share a mutual protection agreement with the Commodore. We keep some of the foreign privateers and navies away, and the pirates generally leave us alone. Very laissez-faire," Dr. Junker said.

"But you haven't joined the Court of the Seventh Array in your husband's stead, nor produced an heir?" Mother asked.

"Stephon's brother, Quentin, possesses the right of succession, therefore I can't join. Unfortunately, he is labeled a 'Person of Spite' in the eyes of Xiao. Until forgiven he cannot claim his rightful position in the outer court. This is why I asked for your help earlier. Without the protection of the Emperor, he had been left vulnerable to the malice of his peers."

Holly sucked air through her teeth, cringing. "That's about as bad as it can get for a noble."

Mother shot Holly a hot side-eye glance. "That label gets thrown around a lot. Of course, a minor irritation to the Emperor can get it hung around your neck. Being shunned by your fellow nobility is the biggest difficulty."

"Indeed," Doctor Junker said. "His peers have kept far away out of fear of being contaminated with his disgrace. Of course, being so tarnished does not liberate you from sending tributes to the Emperor. That only keeps him from punishing you and your people. Puala'Lolo is in good standing. I have made sure of that through my envoys to the court and he still accepts our offerings. Therefore we take comfort that Xiao allows us to exist in his benign neglect."

"I see," Mother said. "Well, in our current circumstances, I guess it never hurts to have a patroness one can call on."

"Patroness? I'm not sure I follow," Dr. Junker's tone was highly tempered.

"We need each other," Mother said. "You want help freeing your brother-in-law, the Baron, Professor Quentin Junker. Winston and Billy Joe require a new beginning. I will continue to need all the allies I can get after this debacle. You and Quentin can make that happen."

"Ah," Dr. Junker said, catching on. "Not blackmail, but an alliance. Perhaps a friendship?"

"That does lessen the chance of betrayal," Mother said with a nod and smile.

"I think we're in the same folder," Dr. Junker nodded.

"My Lady, this looks to be the start of a beautiful friendship," Mother said with a wry smile.

"Am I supposed to get the reference?" Dr. Junker asked.

"Spend time with Winston, and you will," Mother chuckled. "I suspect Professor Junker and Winston will get along just fine."

Mother clapped her hands and rubbed them together eagerly. "Now! We have much to do. Billy Joe, Dolly-"

"Holly," she snarled.

"Whatever," Mother dismissed her protest with a flick of her fingers. "Here's what I need you to do while I make a way for us out of this mess."

5..

"Thank you for the escort back, Billy Joe," Doctor Junker said.

"T'warn't nothin'," he replied with an 'aw shucks' timbre to his voice.

She gave him a tight nod, affirming that they would be ready for the plan. Billy Joe returned it with a two-fingered flick of a salute before heading back forward. Doctor Junker waited till Billy Joe departed before making her next move.

Steeling herself, she crossed the last gap alone. A chorus of "close the door!" followed her exit. She stepped across the cloud-ringed gap to the quarantine container. Even though the faring eddy protected her, a couple of good gusts slapped her like a splash from a fire hose. She held the handholds with a white-knuckled grip and slid the hatch open.

A last gust of wind brought her to a knee as the door closed. She looked up to an arc of dart guns trained on her, the orderlies ready to fire.

"Halt! Identify yourself," the lead orderly commanded.

She held her visitor's pass.

"Baroness Amanda Junker. My brother-in-law is here. That gives me the right to visit with him," she said standing up imperiously, allowing her title to do its work.

"He's over there." The leader spat the words at her.

With all the grace she could muster Doctor Junker pushed through their cordon and wove her way back. Sedated patients slept in spindly, hastily nanofabricated bunks. Quentin lacked one. He was drowsing on the dirty floor, as when she left him to go up front, wrapped in a shiny emergency blanket near the far end. His back was against the wall, legs curled to his chest.

"Quentin," she said, kneeling down next to him.

He gave a small curious groan of awareness and tilted his head, listening intently, but did not open his eyes.

"The Abbey Ferrer has passed away. His jailer is coming to dispose of the body," she said. She spoke in the literary code they had chosen to avert the understanding of those prying ears. Few were familiar with the story of the "Comte de Monte Christo," Quentin's favorite childhood book.

The professor gave a faint smile that emphasized his hollow cheeks and deep eye sockets. Years of neglect from imprisonment had savaged his body. In such times of health and medical miracles, this was deliberate cruelty. His once strong features and limbs hung with sallow limp skin. Her trained eyes saw the mark of forced sedation. He would need intensive recuperation when they got home.

"Mercedes awaits her Edmond's return," she said and smiled. She shot a look over her shoulder to see if anyone was paying attention. The staff had seen her in his room many times before and so ignored her.

"I counted the stones of my cell and called them by name. They bid me farewell," the professor whispered. It took a moment for her to work out what he meant, then she smiled. Quentin was ready as he could be.

Dr. Junker sat down and leaned against the wall with him. Coiling her long skirts around her legs, she leaned against him to help warm his frail body. His hand slipped out of the folds of the blanket like a frightened child, and she took it. All they could do was wait for Mother, Billy Joe, and that dangerous woman to come for them, she thought.

~   ~   ~

Someone's hand gently shook Dr. Junker's shoulder, waking her.

"Yes?" Dr. Junker said, looking up. The quartet of orderlies stood above her and Quentin. Her eyes fell on the open snap on their dart gun holsters.

"Dr. O'Chaudry requires both of you immediately," the first one said politely. He gave her a wane smile designed to calm her suspicion.

"What is this about?" she asked, stretching the sleep out of her limbs. Quentin looked around blearily.

"He didn't say," another said and reached down to help her up. Another helped the professor. "We are to take you both to him right away.

She stood up, dusted herself off from the dirty floor, then reached down to help Quentin to his feet. Inwardly, she cursed Bonavitae for all the sedation they gave him that had him so unsteady. As they began to lead the way back, she remembered the quarantine.

"Wait. He's back there? We don't have any protective gear," Dr. Junker exclaimed.

"Not to worry. The patients are in clean confinement so there is no threat to us," the first orderly explained. With this assurance, she acquiesced. "If you insist. Lead the way."

With the help of the orderlies, the transit was less terrifying this time. The four men transferred them between containers as if they were made of spun sugar.

Once inside the last container, she saw that Dr. O'Chaudry had heavily modified the interior. Wired guards stood watch instead of orderlies. The heavily armed and armored mench stood ready. This was not a quarantine unit. It looked more like one of her husband's splicing labs. What was Bonavitae's real agenda?

"Dr. Junker, thank you for coming so promptly," O'Chaudry crossed the tightly packed space, hand out to greet her.

She pursed her lips and did not accept his hand, keeping hold of her brother-in-law's instead.

"What's this about?" Quentin asked. His eyes flicked around the room, scanning for things important only to him. He clenched Dr. Junker's hand tighter at the sight of his captor, making her wince inwardly at his intense grip.

O'Chaudry pulled back his hand, rubbing his fingers together as if to scrub away the rejection.

"I thought I'd offer accommodations to you in here. They're a bit better than what we have in the other container. We even have a bed free for Quentin."

She said nothing, scrutinizing O'Chaudry like a dangerous reptile.

"Come now," Dr. O'Chaudry said. "This has been a colossal set of unfortunate circumstances. Here you arrive to visit your brother and a Black Void occurs. You cannot blame us for that. These circumstancesare a catastrophe of such magnitude that few ever experience.

"There are several things I blame you for. Ending up in a cargo container because of a natural disaster is not among them," her tone was clipped and formal.

"Civilized comforts go a long way to make such experiences tolerable." O'Chaudry gave her another warm smile. "Sit, and have a drink with me," he enticed.

Dr. Junker's eyes became slits under furrowed brows.

"Do you think me so completely rattled by current events as to forget what is happening? Let alone what you've done to Quentin? You honestly believe I can be handled with cheap, shallow gestures and flattery."

Dr. O'Chaudry let out a snort of frustration and his expression hardened.

"I suppose not, yet I had to make an effort. Trauma caused by disaster often shakes minds into a more agreeable nature. Particularly if they are less emotionally stable. Like your family."

"Ah. Now we dig down into the truth. All this has been personal for you!" Dr. Junker shot back.

He gave a sneer in reply.

"The catacombs," mumbled the professor. "The catacombs of Rome."

Doctor Junker realized Quentin was aware of what was going on. They were caught in the trap she hoped to avoid.

"Case in point. Another one of his insane susurrations," Dr. O'Chaudry sneered. "Orderly, sedate the patient."

"Run, Edmond, run! Your deception is discovered! The keys are out of reach!" Quentin erupted and made a break for the door.

"Orderlies!" O'Chaudry barked. The four wired mench subdued Quentin before he made it three steps. Dr. Amanda attempted to shield him but was deftly removed from the struggle by O'Chaudry.

"No, my lady. We will not be having you interfere anymore," he growled through clenched teeth.

Quentin collapsed a few seconds later. Mumbling strange quotations from a dozen books, he fell asleep under the weight of the drugs. Tears welled in Amanda's eyes. The orderlies picked him up and put his sleeping body in restraints on the open bed.

"What... what are you going to do?" she stammered.

O'Chaudry walked over to a small computer station mounted beneath the container's load monitor. A wired caninoid with several sophisticated computers sat beside it and gave a nod to Dr. O'Chaudry.

"I am solving several of my problems at the same time. Pardon me a moment." He ran his hand through his slick black hair and looked up at the comm lens and gave the gesture to begin to the caninoid.

"Who is this?" came Holly's voice through the speaker.

His tight sour smirk materialized. "This is Dr. O'Chaudry. Put whoever's in charge on the comm. I assume it's this dataoid of yours, Mother, correct?"

"A holo-display burst into life and projected a miniature image of Mother instead of a readout.

"What do you want?" she demanded.

"I am taking charge of this voyage," O'Chaudry declared, his smile loosening a fraction.

"Like purg you are," Mother shot back.

"We are changing course to Carmadon 5 instead of Nova Tortuga." His tone like a drawn sword.

The image of Mother paused as she whipped through the ship's navigation system.

"That's a high-security corporate zone! What makes you think we'll risk our lives and allow you to deliver us into your company's clearly irresponsible hands?" But then she saw Dr. Junker.

"That's right. I have your ally and her brother-in-law. Unless you want something horrible to happen to them, you will do as I command." O'Chaudry looked like the cat who ate the bird.

Mother pinched the bridge of her nose as if in great spiritual pain.

Dr. O'Chaudry smugly piled on. "I suspect you are already calculating a way to have your cake and eat it too, so let me save you the time. You aren't going to be able to use the gravity fields to subdue us, because we have hostages. That's on top of the hundreds of innocents you could doom to the slow death of floating away. I doubt you're like several of my patients who are capable of committing mass slaughter."

Dr. O'Chaudry's eyes danced with vicious savor. "Furthermore, you do not have any combat force of which to speak. Your pilot is down with synapse burn which means you can't try any fancy aerial acrobatic tricks of. That mechoid loadmaster is not a combat model. The truck stop whore isn't capable enough to subdue my nurses, let alone my orderlies. We're in breathable airspace, so you can't knock us out with a low air pressure pocket or toxic gas."

Mother glowered at the administrator. It lacked all her impressive gravitas when she stood only seven inches tall.

"I should also mention that your tug's computers are severely compromised. Thus, we have taken control of the coupling system. Any attempt to cut us adrift will result in that tug engaging in an emergency stop. Our full unmodified mass will free-fall straight through you. Yes, that will leave us drifting ourselves, but we will have power and an emergency beacon, while you will be dead."

"And you took control of our outside comms," Mother observed.

"Of course. We can't have you tattling to some party who might decide to meddle."

A frustrated tear rolled down Dr. Amanda's cheek, her hands clenched into fists. Everything had flown apart in such a short time.

"So there you are. Powerless to say no to my orders," Dr. O'Chaudry stated, spreading his arms wide with a satisfied smile on his face.

"Carmadon 5 you said?" Mother seethed.

"Correct."

"It seems we have no choice," Mother surrendered.

"How long will it take to arrive?" O'Chaudry asked.

"About eighteen to nineteen hours according to my best estimate," the caninoid said.

"You don't know?" Dr. O'Chaudry's growled.

"Of course he doesn't know for sure," Mother interjected. "You said it yourself. Our computers are compromised, maxed out, and need a lot of repair and data maintenance. This is about as clear an answer as you're going to get. Eighteen hours-ish, barring any complications with our transit."

"Don't forget, I'm watching you," Dr. O'Chaudry warned.

Mother snapped off the comm leaving Dr. Amanda alone and terrified.

6.

"Now step up. That's it. Good job," Holly encouraged as she guided Winston to finish another set of ladder climbs from the keel airlock gangway.

The holoprojector burst to life and Holly let out a squeak of surprise almost losing her grip on Winston. Mother materialized.

"Don't forget, I'm watching you!" Mother growled, twisting her expression, mocking Dr. O'Chaudry's last words. "I'm watching you!" She parroted again and began stalking around the cab. "I'll give you something to watch soon enough, smart-ass."

"You scared the cheis out of me!" Holly shouted.

Mother glared back at the assassin for daring to yell at her and blanched. Her jaw dropped when she realized what Holly had been doing with Winston.

"What do you think-? He'll fall! Are you trying to make things worse?" Mother protested.

"No. He won't," Holly yelled. "I've been beneath him the whole time, and it's not like he's too heavy for me to handle."

Mother arched an eyebrow. "I guess that could be considered an expert opinion from a woman who spends lots of time with men on top of her."

Holly gritted her teeth. She took Winston to his pilot's seat and sloppily dropped him in before wheeling on the sassy dataoid. "It's been working! The larger range of movements sped up his recovery. He's mumbling now and again and walking almost unassisted!" she shouted back.

Billy Joe woke up and came out of his rack.

"What's going on, Mother?" Billy Joe asked.

She gave the indu a withering stare. Now him too? She didn't have time for this. She split her mental processes in two so she could multi-task, her primary consciousness dove into the *Sierra*

Madre's servers, while the daughter copy took over her hologram's interactions with Holly.

Mother's primary self found herself in a factory without end or purpose. Huge industrial machines surrounded her like a mad tuneless cathedral of smoke, sparks and noise.

She grimaced, assaulted by the stench and cacophony before changing the simulation settings. Then came blessed, scentless silence. Using a secret command override on Billy Joe she yanked his consciousness into the simulation with her for a private talk.

Billy Joe spun around in confusion as he spawned in the instance with her. "What? How?" He floundered for a second as he processed what happened to him. "Rather rude, Mother. Even by your standards," he said with a shaming shake of his head.

She opened her mouth to deliver a sour quip but closed it. He was right. She nodded with a cleansing sigh.

"I'm sorry, Bubby. I didn't mean to take my frustration out on you. We don't have time for ruffled feathers." She realized how rare even a qualified apology was from her, and Billy Joe's face showed it. "So this is how you spend your downtime, Bubby?" she asked, changing the subject. A hydraulic press crushed out a giant gear next to her.

"I find it soothing," Billy Joe said with a shoulder shrug. "Why'd you drag me in here?" he asked, clearly still cross at the liberty she had taken with his code.

"We needed a private talk. O'Chaudry's taken hostages and seized control of most of the *Sierra Madre's* computer network. And on top of that cheis buffet, he is demanding we re-route to Carmadon 5."

"Y'all think it's safe to talk in here if he's taken control of our network?" Billy Joe fretted.

"Yes, I do. He may think that Dober-Man he's got working for him is some top-notch hacker, but he's not a dataoid. That's like sending a dog to catch a shark in the water." Mother's smirk was a thing of super-villain perfection. "He sees what I want him to see, and I've taken several precautions to keep your personal drives safe.

I'm certain they're more interested in the show going on in the cab with my duplicate avatar arguing with Holly. That hacker's attention is focused hard on her and her bountiful pontoons. Caninoid or not, he's still male. Let's see who can figure out *that* Turing test first! As for you, your body is watching the two of us fight with fretful looks. You're welcome."

"That's fine and dandy, but how is this helping our situation?" Billy Joe complained.

"We need to do two things, and do them fast. First, I must find a way to secure all the *Sierra Madre's* data networks. Second, we must pull together and rescue our new patroness. This should put another big feather in our cap if we pull it off," Mother said with a smile.

"But don't he have a whole mess o' armed guards and stuff?" Billy Joe said. "In case you didn't notice, I'm not a combat mechoid."

"Billy Joe," Mother said, coming close to him. She patted his cheek tenderly. "You can't remember, but I know precisely what you are and what you can do."

"What's that supposed to mean?" the indu fidgeted, gliding back away from her at a snail's pace, eyes wide with worry.

Mother winked at him.

This activated a long-dormant key in Billy Joe's code.

A set of deeply sequestered data, implanted when Billy Joe was fresh off the nanofab, went active.

She watched the code override and begin updating parts of Billy Joe's operating system. His avatar froze, pixelated, then flickered as his operating systems rebooted. Mother smiled in satisfaction. "Don't you worry, Bubby. You've just changed the balance of power. When you're done rebooting, I'll see you on the outside." She logged out. It was time to put the third part of her plan into action.

7.

The *Sierra Madre* obeyed O'Chaudry's hacker's commands and kept course through a thick dust layer. It hissed and crackled against the canopy and the sky went from deep orange to red as they descended deeper into the Dream, leaving the hot upper layers behind.

"All right, all right! You did what you thought was best!" Mother shouted. She turned her holographic back on Holly to gaze out of the canopy, squinting at the diamondoid glass panes. "O'Chaudry's hacker is a pinhead," she growled. "This dust must be etching the canopy. That's going to require replacement or professional polishing."

"Wha?" Holly grunted, perplexed by the conversation change.

Mother fired off a fast text to Holly titled:

"Read Me Before You Say Another Stupid Word!"

Mother turned and knelt down next to Winston. It was for show, but she knew bionts forgot how dataoids worked if they mimicked their behavior. Never give a sucker an even break. Winston's eyes slowly blinked in an unsynchronized fashion, like a cat in a sunbeam. He was mumbling the "Tadercrisps" jingle to himself.

Holly gave an irritated snort as she read the title on her cybercomm. She flopped down in the navigator's seat that she had adopted as her own for the voyage and read the message. Her expression tightened as she read Mother's summation of their current predicament.

"You want me to keep walking Winston or not?" she asked out loud.

"I think you managed to get yet another man over the hump, as it were," Mother snipped.

"You know… There are nicer ways to say that," Holly grumbled, sick of the attitude. With a sigh, she turned on her music and started texting Mother through her cybercomm.

~   ~   ~

NIGHTSHADE1: "So, what do we want to do about our new status as hostages?"

MOTHERADMIN: "Take a moment to look at our flight plan on the pilot displays. Do you see the *Sierra Madre* headed to Carmadon 5?

NIGHTSHADE1: "Confirmed. Straight shot, basic auto avoidance, ignoring all approved flight lanes. If unlucky, we might attract some Imperial attention. This course should take 14 hours at current speed."

MOTHERADMIN: "I had a feeling that Caninoid was wrong. Unfortunately, I'm unable to ascertain if Bonavitae Corporate has been informed of this situation. If they have, they might send out long-range fighters or an airship to secure our capture. We should assume so and an escort will arrive in less than half that time. Five or six hours at soonest.

NIGHTSHADE1: "Then we need to move. But if he runs the ship and threatened to splatter us if we don't play along, what do you expect me to do? I'm content to hang tight and fill out a job application with them."

MOTHERADMIN: "I doubt their brothel has an opening. Tell me, do you enjoy your ability to have free thought?

NIGHTSHADE1: "What's that supposed to mean?"

MOTHERADMIN: "These people strip brains like stolen aircars. They do so for the pleasure and profit of very powerful sentients. You're not a potential employee or contractor. You're a loose thread. Have you not realized that yet? You can't behng your way to safety on this one."

NIGHTSHADE1: "Are you this bitchy because you aren't real, or just a personality mod of someone's nasty mother-in-law? Fine. What are we going to do then?"

MOTHERADMIN: "Billy Joe is going to rescue the hostages."

NIGHTSHADE1: "How? With a torque wrench? A pallet jack? He's a BJB model! He programmed for cargo handling and basic maintenance on this tub, not security!"

MOTHERADMIN: "Five minutes ago, that may have been true, but not anymore. He's not standing around looking cute because he can't do anything. He's waiting for orders."

NIGHTSHADE1: "And what the purg do you expect me to do?"

MOTHERADMIN: "You will do your best to be a rather flamboyant threat. You're going to draw off whatever muscle O'Chaudry has. While you are keeping their attention focused outside, Billy Joe will use that opening to subdue our captors inside. He will rescue Doctor and Professor Junker. My job will be to make sure that nobody gets a distress call out or makes any 'mistakes' with the gravity drive. I don't need you blown off the hull, or for us to get pulped.

NIGHTSHADE1: "Go outside? Are you nuts? What kinds of weapons do they have? Thanks to your idiot indu I don't even have my two pistols!"

MOTHERADMIN: "He'll give them back! You have armor and both pistols. Allegedly you're an excellent assassin if we believe you. So suck it up, go out there, and be as lethal as you are distracting!"

NIGHTSHADE1: "Are you going to be able to slow this tug down to a speed where I won't be torn off the hull? Otherwise, that's a hard no!"

MOTHERADMIN: "It's already being done by that pinhead hacker as we speak. I will make sure it stays that way till we have control again. I can't be losing you before Bubby gets our new friends free and maybe chops Dr. O'Chaudry into canimorph kibble as a bonus."

NIGHTSHADE1: "What? Why didn't he do this sooner?"

MOTHERADMIN: "He couldn't. I hadn't removed the civilian safety interlocks blocking him. I fixed that and installed military-grade software drivers for his nanosand. Billy Joe is now as dangerous as one of Xiao's waroids."

NIGHTSHADE1: "Then you don't need me, or better still put him outside. He can suction to the hull and I'll go up the middle."

MOTHERADMIN: "Him I trust to not slaughter innocent non-combatants. He may be able to function as a waroid, but he still retains his full morality. That includes a desire to preserve life if he can. His list of options on how he manages that just got… longer. The less said about my trust in you, the less you'll cry yourself to sleep tonight."

NIGHTSHADE1: "And if I refuse to play along?"

MOTHERADMIN: "Do not entertain the hope that I won't cut my losses in this debacle! Things go too sideways and I am only a spawned avatar. I can abandon you all to whatever fate O'Chaudry has planned if I must!"

NIGHTSHADE1: "You'd be killing your own people!"

MOTHERADMIN: Yes, it will be sad to lose Winston and Billy Joe. I've grown fond of them over the years, but if I have to let you all die or get lobotomized in some mad scientist laboratory to protect myself, you best remember that's option number two for me! Now, are you in or out? Clock's ticking!"

NIGHTSHADE1: "Nahq it. I'm in."

MOTHERADMIN: "Good. Now let me give Bubby his marching orders, and you two can get on with it. When he leaves the tug to go back, you go too. I'll set the stage and make sure they notice you outside."

8.

The first indication that Dr. O'Chaudry's plan had gone awry was a mobile therapy station gently bumping into the container's bulkhead. He looked up in surprise as a building shudder rattled the container and all its contents. He shot an accusatory gaze toward Dr. Junker. She clung to the bed of her sedated and restrained brother-in-law. She looked just as confused as O'Chaudry felt.

The orderlies instinctively gripped their dart guns and fought to keep from sliding along the floor.

With a snarl, O'Chaudry wheeled on his IT admin, "Did they break control?"

The caninoid flipped through his screen tabs and shrugged. "Doesn't look like it, but I'm getting alerts from the tug. Something's going on with the fans."

Dr. O'Chaudry opened up the comm to the *Sierra Madre's* cab. Winston's face filled the screen. His unfocused eyes wandered and he babbled like a drunk, unable to speak anything but repetitive nonsense.

"Yes, Doctor?" Mother said cutting the connection to her. O'Chaudry wanted to gag from her sickeningly sweet demeanor. His trained eye considered her choreographed response. Oh, yes, he thought. She knew what was going on. "What's happening with the grav fans?" he snapped.

"It appears that all the strain put on the motors recently has caused a gravitational flutter. We thought you were aware of it since you took over the controls," Mother explained. Her obsequious customer service demeanor infuriated him further. She was toying with him.

Dr. O'Chaudry muted his mic and turned back to his IT admin to verify the claim. "Well?"

"I'm not a pilot. It could be true. A flutter would slow us down and give a vibration," he said

with a shrug. There was another lurch and the
Sierra Madre fell into subsonic speeds and
continued slowing down.

"Thaaaaaaat's not right," the Caninoid said.
He looked apprehensively about the container as
if he could see what was going on through the
hull.

"Are they doing this? I warned them!" Dr.
O'Chaudry yelled.

"Doesn't look like it, sir. But I am getting a new
alarm." the hacker said.

"What now?" the administrator half-whined in
frustration.

"A freeze warning?" the doberman caninoid
scratched his ear nervously. "How could there be
ice here?"

Mother continued to smile sweetly on the
comms.

Dr. O'Chaudry unmuted the channel. "Are
you seeing this on your instruments?" he
demanded.

"Now that you mention it," Mother said, dripping with false surprise. "I do seem to see a little red indicator for a problem."

"What's a freeze warning?" Dr. O'Chaudry's temple was throbbing.

"The combination of gravitational flutter and your chosen flight path is coating the grav fans in stone. These dust clouds are precipitating out, forming a crust around the gravity projectors. A typical hazard that is dealt with by proper course correction. Something an actual pilot would avoid. Thanks to the flutter, the condensate has become thick enough to interfere with the fans," Mother explained.

Dr. O'Chaudry wanted to punch someone. Anyone. "You did this," he seethed, accusing Mother.

"No. This is your doing. Poor airmanship on whoever you have piloting back there. Either the autopilot must have been overridden, or the sensors are unable to detect the threat." Mother stared back, her face a hard slate.

"Us?" O'Chaudry blanched.

"Yes, you. We're your captives up here. You've made that quite clear. Our instruments are locked out, and can only watch the readouts."

O'Chaudry hit the mute again and glared a question to his IT admin demanding verification.

"Sir, I told you, I'm not a pilot! I did what you told me. Locked them out and set up our course. Their autopilot does the rest," the caninoid gestured with agitated flaps of his arms. "She's not lying about the shape this tug is in. It's bad. Someone hacked the cheis out of its systems before we got here. The rest of the space on the drives is packed full with that nahq dataoid's avatar. The best I can do is check the fans. Maybe their auto-tuning systems will still work and I can re-calibrate them. But no matter what, the stone's gotta be chipped off. Until that's done we're dead in the sky." To prove his point he spun his monitor around to show the fan's status.

An exterior camera revealed thick stalagmites poking out of the grav fans like cartoon exhaust. The stone slowly grew over the fan's surface, getting longer and longer. The bigger the deposits became, the more they decelerated.

"We have to shut the fans down the fans and get someone out there to smash the rock off to clear 'em," the hacker stated.

Another fan's freeze alarm went off. The caninoid swiveled the camera to see another fan filling with stone. While O'Chaudry watched, a pair of sexy legs flashed past the camera.

"What was that?" he barked. The hacker zoomed out and tracked where the legs went. Holly stopped and looked down at the camera. She gave a chilling imperious pose, drew one of her pistols, and blew it out.

Dr. O' Chaudry was slack-jawed.

"Are you still there?" Mother's voice came over his comm.

"What?" he exploded at her image. When she didn't react, he saw the comm was muted. He recomposed himself and turned the microphone back on. "I'm still here. What is it? Why is that whore on the hull? How'd she get guns?"

"It might interest you to know that our passenger has decided to take matters into her own hands. Despite my best efforts, she's become rather excitable. You've given her the impression you plan to do her grave harm on Carmadon 5," Mother explained.

"Why didn't you stop her?" O'Chaudry demanded.

"I lacked the means! Our mechoid is in a shutdown cycle. As a hologram, I had no physical way to stop her, so she took the opportunity. Not to mention, I was also attending to other matters," she gave him a sour accusing look.

"You should have sealed the airlocks," O'Chaudry snapped.

"You saw how damaged our computers are. *She* is the one who caused most of that, and with your IT puppy, you have control," Mother accused.

Dr. O'Chaudry rubbed his face in anguish.

"Regrettably, I believe she intends to kill you to keep from going to your facility. Do you have enough security to defend yourself from a wired assassin?"

"She's not a prostitute?" O'Chaudry's words felt small but incredibly heavy in his mouth.

"Oh! No," Mother said with a disapproving air. "Despite her penchant for dressing like a sex doll, she's in fact a special military operator of some sort. Perhaps a freelance assassin, I never determined. Regardless, she's a henchwoman for someone very powerful."

Sweat beaded on Dr. O'Chaudry's brow.

"She wasn't part of your crew?" he demanded.

"No," Mother purred. "She joined us as a previous employer's representative. We were on our way to being rid of her when the Black Void altered our plans. That means, in her eyes, *you* are probably as expendable as we are. Allow me to cheer my support for your efforts in disposing of this threat to all of us. Rah! Rah!"

"You were hostages when you rescued us? Why did you even come?" Dr. O'Chaudry's hand went to his forehead to rub away the throbbing headache.

"That's far too long of an answer than you have time for. Think of it as we were previously engaged at the time of your rescue. But, anyhoo… I shouldn't distract you from your more immediate crisis of dealing with her," Mother gloated. "*Sierra Madre* out."

The connection cut off, and all Dr. O'Chaudry could do was gape at the disconnect icon.

Another camera tracked Holly as she strutted toward his container. Her neon orange hair streamed in the wind, her eyes glowing red.

"Sir?" the IT admin hazarded, "what do you want us to do?"

"Spin the ship. Play crack the whip. Anything! Just get her off the hull!" Dr. O'Chaudry screamed. He slammed his fists down on a therapy table and massaged his temples.

The wolf splice cleared his throat and whispered, "It seems that we're now cut off. Besides, the motors are clogged with stone. I couldn't maneuver the tug if I wanted to. Every attempt I make to re-establish control results in getting spammed with rude gestures denial memes."

Dr. O'Chaudry looked at Doctor Junker and the professor . A steely resolve welled up within him.

"Re-establish what control you can," he ordered to the caninoid, then turned to an orderly. "We'll get our secret projects out on the hull. Let's test them out by having them kill that woman," his voice, ice cold.

"Yes, sir," an orderly replied. He went to one of the six medical cylinders, tapped in some codes, and engaged the activation sequence.

A few seconds later, the translucent oval door glowed with light and chimed it had completed the revivification of its subject. There was a pop and soft gasp of air as it equalized pressure. White condensation puffed out as the door opened. A hand, its skin shiny black with bright yellow spots and oversized webbed fingers, emerged to grip the edge.

"Don't they look marvelous?" Dr. O'Chaudry admired.

An ominous low croaking sound was his only reply.

9.

"Come on, Mother," Holly said into her cybercomm. "You said you'd make sure they'd come after me. I'm taking a slow stroll for effect, and still nothing?"

"Trust me," Mother replied. "They're all riled up. Expect them any second now."

Holly hopped across to the fifth container. Even with the comparatively mild wind of fifty miles per hour, a simple jump was not easy. Her landing was a bit iffy. Even with all the gyro compensation her stiletto-heeled boots gave, she fell to her hands and knees. There was no cat-like "I meant to do that" way of making her fall look deliberate. She was grateful for her Bumblebee flight harness.

"Klutz," she chided herself and took great care getting to her feet as a side gust gave an extra nudge.

An ominous low rumbling croak came from the gap behind her. Unable to recognize the odd sound was, she crept over to the end of the containers and took a cautious look between them.

Four giant amphiboids who had been climbing up the sides of the container hull stared back. They were almost twice her size. Giant frog-like heads with oversized mouths glistening with slime grinned viciously at her. Their black rubbery skin was a patchwork of shockingly bright, yellow, orange and red blotches.

"Behnging purg!" Holly screamed and threw herself away from the edge. Two sticky tongues zipped by her like pink cannonballs on bungee cords. A wind gust tossed her half the length of the container, much farther than she anticipated. Once her slide stopped, she drew a pistol and aimed. The creatures came over the top in a wave and crawled with purpose toward her.

She opened fire. Three shots exploded one of the amphiboids in a viscous blast of mucus and gore. The wind threw the spray all over her. The other frog horrors tumbled and rolled with gooey slaps. Fingers and toes stuck to the surface of the container like suction cups. They slunk toward her with boneless weaving movements.

Holly wiped off her face. Her lips started to tingle, then began to burn and spread. She looked at the slime that covered her hand. Her internal medical systems jangled alarms as her face started to go numb.

Little red warning lights appeared in the corner of her vision. The offal spray contained dangerous neurotoxins, digestive acids and other chemical threats. Her implanted poison nanofabricators began to search their databases for the correct antivenin. Other medical implants kicked into gear. Adrenaline, antihistamines, anti-inflammatories and other neutralizing substances flooded her body.

Another growling croak came from behind her. She looked over her shoulder to see two more of the amphiboids crawling over the top, boxing her in!

"Ha ha!" one of the two new ambushers laughed. "Too late for you, little lady! We're poisonous like you can't imagine. There's never been anything as lethal as our touch. Surrender and we'll kill you quick!" the amphiboid on point shouted over the roaring wind.

"Holy cheis!" Holly breathed. "You talk?"

"A'course we can talk! We're soldiers, not animals!" the other ambusher shouted, giving a haughty grimace.

"Well, purg. The things people won't do to themselves these days," she sighed and opened fire on the offended amphiboid. Her shots missed as he juked out of the way of her aim.

The other ambusher spat his huge pink blob of a tongue at her. It smacked into the pistol like a wad of chewed gum, enveloping her hands and weapon. The elastic tongue tightened its grip and sprang back, pulling the gun with it. Holly fought to hold on to her weapon as the tongue jerked her onto her belly with a hard landing. The pistol went off and exploded the amphiboid's gooey tongue tip into disgusting streamers of meat and slime. More neurotoxin splashed her face and the pistol flew off into the sky.

The wounded amphiboid gave a terrifying gurgling scream. It clutched its bloody mouth and ducked back down between the containers.

The remaining four frog creatures pounced on her. She curled up into a tight ball to protect her neck and face. The toxin effects grew more intense as a painful numbness filled her brain making her woozy and more disoriented. Nano-cybernetic implants took over her body's compromised motor control and autonomic nervous system. Emergency filters worked overtime to protect her brain.

Externally, Holly was being savaged like a pack of hyenas on a zebra carcass. Needle-sharp nail tips tried to scratch through her smartex armor. They tried to lift the stiff pandifico plates looking for soft spots to stab. The armor stretched and sprung her about. She slammed hard against the hull. Fists clubbed her non-stop. Powerful kicks to her reinforced ribs and vertebrae did not succeed.

Holly was thrown onto her back. A pair of the creatures worked to pull her arms away from her clenched body to expose her head and neck, but her supercharged muscles would not give. She did not scream or panic as she absorbed the beating.

"Ahh!" one of the amphiboids yelled, frustrated. "Let's just throw her over the side and be done with her!"

"We're moving too slow," a second one said. "She'd just use that flight rig and we'd be fighting her again in no time. Gotta kill her first."

"Let the poison do its job. Till then we play Sokker with her body," another croaked.

Through the tiny gap in her forearms, she saw the now tongueless amphiboid crawl up to the scrum. Blood dribbled from its mouth.

"Ah wah wegenff," the wounded frog splice gargled.

"What?" one croaked

"He wants revenge," a third translated. "Can't say I blame you, brother! That's gotta hurt!"

"Weff pway feep foophing," the wounded amphiboid said.

Holly caught a glimpse of his bulging eyes locking onto the second pistol on her hip.

"Skeet shooting? Oh yeah!"

"Love it!"

"Do her with her own gun!"

"Git it!"

With one frog splice pulling each limb, they lifted her off the hull, holding her between them like a crate.

Far off in her poison-soaked perception, she felt the catch release open. This was the best opening she'd get.

Holly jack-hammered both legs straight into the two amphiboids holding her ankles. One leg punched clear through the amphiboid's gut on her right, like a polearm. Her thigh becoming trapped in his abdomen. She hacked away the chest cavity of the other with her stiletto heel, peeling half the rib cage open. The kick threw his body into the sky and it fell away from the train of containers like the body of a hit-and-run.

She wrenched her right hand free and lashed out. Her hammer fist pulped the grabby wounded amphiboid's skull with a slaughterhouse crunch. Without a flinch, his body dropped to the hull.

Holly found herself awkwardly twisted. She was half stretched between her caught leg and the amphiboid who held her left arm. She reached across her body for her remaining pistol.

The world went black and sticky. One of the amphiboids had swallowed her by the head! Its powerful mouth bound her arms to her chest, constricting like a straitjacket. Each gulp drawing her deeper into its gullet.

Internal alarms strobed warnings as the small tears in her armor leaked more, different, poisons in from multiple points. Her blood oxygen was dropping fast. Despite her nanowired nerves, her voluntary muscles were seizing. The poison filters were unable to keep up.

A last sickening swallow and her legs slid in as the frog splice swallowed Holly alive. She tried desperately to kick her way out, but her movements had become mere wiggles and twitches.

"Hey, look! Ha! She's still trying to break free! You can see her squirm through my belly!" the amphiboid who swallowed her bragged.

"Seems like getting these splice mods done was worth it," the other crowed. Its rumbling voice was muffled by the flesh of the one who swallowed her.

"Bonavitae really knows its stuff," the last of the trio agreed.

"I dunno. She seemed to handle poisons that shoulda killed her in seconds."

"She's a nanoborg or somethin'. Probably take a while to overwhelm whatever implants she got."

"Yeah, but still."

"I'm going to need tools to break that stone off. Best go get some from up front. Good chance they have them in the tractor," the other grumbled.

"You go ahead," Holly felt the one who ate her say. "I'm- urp -kinda full at the moment and it's a li- mburrrup- little hard to move."

Holly's "Low Oxygen" countdown warning had begun. She was almost out of time. Her right hand slithered around her waist to find the pistol grip but lacked the strength to draw it from the holster. The tight muscles of the amphiboid's stomach still bound her weakening body.

"You do that, mench," the unencumbered frog splice said. "See if your new stomach can dissolve that cute little snack."

Holly could feel the amphiboid dragging himself back toward a container hatch. Stomach acid began to work on her face with a growing burn.

A green alert appeared in her warning menu. Her toxin filters found a solution and began churning out antivenin. She might make it after all -if she didn't suffocate first.

Holly wedged her finger inside the holster and hooking a fingernail on the trigger. She tugged with all the strength she had left.

The report wasn't as deafening as she expected. It felt like a slap throughout her body as the round blew out the holster and popped the amphiboid like a water balloon, blowing them both over the side of the hull and into the air.

There was a horrifying and thrilling rush in her belly as Holly realized she was in free fall. The antivenin finally overcame enough of the neurotoxin to return a little of her strength. With a weak shove, she pulled her head out of the amphiboid corpse.

With a disgusting, heaving retch, she blew the mucus and stomach juices out of her mouth and nose. A gasp of air never tasted so sweet. She would survive being beaten, poisoned, suffocated and eaten alive. Now to see if she could get back on board.

The dark tunnel of oxygen starvation that had ringed her vision cleared up. She scanned all around for the *Sierra Madre*. Far away, Holly saw her shrinking into the distance as it flew away. No way could her Bumblebee catch up, even as slow as she was moving. Holly was doomed to fall forever in the endless Dream with a corpse of a frog splice as her only company.

Lovely.

10..

The new drivers and combat software had changed Billy Joe's nanosand into a suite of deadly options. The first orderly refused to surrender and drew his gun and was sliced in twain from crown to pelvis. Everyone else gave up peacefully after that. Billy Joe picked up all the weapons and sedated the rest of the container.

"Mother, I'm not so sure this is a good change for my life," Billy Joe mumbled, blood dripping down his chassis.

"You're doing fine, Bubby," Mother encouraged. She fried another brute force attempt to crack the security seals that protected her code. "Just keep going. Naqh! This hacker O'Chaudry has is a crafty one!" she griped.

"What's that, Mother?" Billy Joe asked as he forced the lock on the next container hatch. Darts bounced off his outer shell. One of the orderlies made a dash for an electro stunner and Billy Joe clipped him in half with a shears-tipped pseudopod.

"That IT admin has decided a better defense was a good offense and the server's full of holes!" Mother grumbled and created a fourth capture maze to slow down the brute force attacks. "He hasn't gotten me on the ropes yet, but if you don't get through to him soon, I'm going to have to shut down comms."

"Yes, ma'am! Going as fast as I can, but they're still strugglin', and that's slowin' me down a mite," Billy Joe said, crossing the gap to the next container. The surviving orderlies and nurses saw the giant shears swaying back and forth like a snake ready to strike and they gave up. Billy Joe tranqed them up and went straight through to the next hatch.

"This is like having a knife fight in a shower stall! Ahh!" Mother screamed as she lost control of some of the *Sierra Madre's* systems.

"Look out!" she warned Billy Joe as he was about to cross over the gap. He flinched back in the nick of time as the gravity couplers faded. The containers bumped into each other with a deafening bang.

"That nearly crushed me!" Billy Joe shouted to her.

"Give me a second, and I'll have the coupling chain back in my control," Mother gave a static-filled grunt. "Where'd this guy get these bots? It's like a drone swarm!"

"I'm going through," Billy Joe said and slid his nanite fingers into the seal of the next hatch, wrenching it open.

"Got it!" Mother said, and the gravity couplers pushed the gap back into their proper distance. Billy Joe flowed through and was instantly attacked. It seemed as if the orderlies had gotten the word to use electro stunners.

He returned fire with the dart guns confiscated in previous containers, spraying the container with four tendril-mounted pistols at the same time while moving further inside. Those not in light armor went down in seconds. The orderlies tried to counter with stabs from their spear-like stunners, but Billy Joe bobbed around like a cork in stormy seas, slashing with whip-like arms any orderly who got close enough to fry his systems. They were smashed to paste. Once he pacified the occupants, the three dozen patients and nurses lay in sleeping piles on the floor with the corpses of the orderlies who refused to surrender.

"How you holding up, Mother?" Billy Joe asked as he reached the hatch to the last container. "You have everything under control if I open the door? I don't want to set off no doomsday device he rigged up to kill us all."

Mother didn't reply. Billy Joe checked his connection again. "Mother, you got'cher ears on, good buddy?" He hoped the ancient hail would tick her off enough to answer even if busy.

Still nothing.

Should he go through the door or wait till Mother responded? What was she facing on her end? Was it too late?

Her comm keyed open. "Trouble-" then a bunch of lag stretching out the words with the interference. "-ab!" the signal broke off again "-inst-" then the comm channel closed.

11..

Winston groaned. Blaring buzzers pestered him to wake up like an alarm clock that was personally angry at him for slapping 'snooze' too many times. His hand drifted to his temple and tried to stop the swelling throb.

"Mmmmng…" he moaned. "Shut up! Ow…" he hissed. It was like touching a sunburn.

"Wut the purg?" he muttered, pain clearing his mind enough to crack open his eyes. The cab was like an arcade run amok. Lights and sounds bombarded him. Warnings he'd never seen before screamed for attention. Gingerly, he started opening up his control screens.

The *Sierra Madre* was nearly floating dead in the sky. All four grav fans were over three-quarters clogged by condensates. Her reactor was down to 18% fuel. Most computer systems were down despite operating at almost full processing power. The automatic economy systems had kicked on due to a major virus outbreak in its networks. Then there was a massive data structure consuming over 80% of all memory. Plus an outside data threat attacking his tug like a swarm of killer bees.

It was almost too much to believe.

"Bubby? How long have I been out?" Winston gasped. He received no response. "Bubby?" Still no answer.

He looked around the cab but found himself alone. He turned to the comms. "Bubby! Where are you?" he shouted into the link.

"Hoss?" came the surprised reply scrambled by a wall of lag.

"What is going on around here?" Winston demanded. Methodically, he silenced the alarms and began forced shutdowns of all non-essential systems. He tried firing up the emergency rescue data protocols. "Are we under some sort of cyberattack?"

"Y'all could say that! Are you in control of all our systems, Hoss? I can't raise Mother," Billy Joe asked.

"Yeah. Wait!" Winston froze, hands hanging in mid-command over his touchscreens. "Why wouldn't I be?"

"That's a long talk we cain't do right now. Do you have full control up there?" Billy Joe was pushier than Winston ever heard before.

He tapped a quick request for diagnostics. Half of his controls were being run out of the last container through the data umbilical. Some sumbitch had back-hacked his system!

"No, naqh it! Someone snaked my authority! You get back there and deal with them. Wait a second! Wait, wait, wait for me," Winston yelled, and threw himself out of the pilot's seat. "I'mina bust their access,and it's gonna be a bit startling." He ran into the engineering passage and unlocked the bypass cabinet. The system boards revealed a plethora of tripped breakers and locked-out controls.

"Bubby, why were you trying to comm Mother?" Winston asked as he checked their relative airspeed. It was under 30 miles per hour. Just coasting despite the fans running at max power. Good. He could do this.

"She's downloaded her avatar to here cuz we're up cheis creek and needed operational security."

"What?!" Winston exploded. "She knows how dangerous that is!"

"Hoss, it's done. She's here. We don't got time to talk about it and that's that! Do what you're gonna do, fast, so I can deal with this behnger in the back. Our lives are on the line," Billy Joe pleaded.

There was a knock on the container access hatch window.

Winston turned to look and saw a giant frog eye looking in.

"Hey! Unlock the door, fella, and maybe you'll live through this!" The amphiboid's muffled order was punctuated with a dull croak.

"Xiao on a cracker!" Winston screamed. He yanked three levers at the same time: the master data bypass, the data rescue system with its clean software copy and the gravity brakes.

The action had three distinct effects on the *Sierra Madre*.

First, all data connections to and from every source external to the tug were severed physically. The external cyberattack alarms ceased.

Secondly, the rescue backup system was connected to the corrupted data cores and began working its magic. A new set of amber and green icons blinked to life while several red ones went out.

Last, the drives went to true neutral. The *Sierra Madre* came to an abrupt dead stop in the sky.

The gravity couplers went to emergency independent mode and buffered the hard stop, compressing together. The containers hit their bumper plates hard, but not enough to damage themselves or the tug.

There was a terror-filled croak of alarm that ceased with a sudden splattering crunch.

A hard shudder rippled through the cab, knocking Winston off his feet and sending him flying out of the engineering passage, skidding on his side into the cab.

The impact shattered large amounts of stone condensate off the grav fans and a cloud of marbled stalactites and gravel flew past the nose of the *Sierra Madre*.

Winston crawled a few feet over to the pilot seat, laughing in giddy triumph. He hoped Bubby had been ready for that and not between any of the containers. Still on the floor, he reached over and fired up the fan-cleaning cycle. That would oscillate the gravity planes inside the fans causing them to vibrate. It would break up the rest of the crystalline deposits in minutes and they could start heading to a safe port. Hopefully, one where they could do extensive repairs.

The familiar buzzing vibration rose, thrumming the frame as it intensified. Winston turned his attention to the *Sierra Madre's* data systems. That massive data structure must be Mother. Someone had turned the Tug's anti-virus on her like she was the threat. Winston paused the program and white-listed the massive block of data he suspected was Mother.

The comm on the dash started blinking. He keyed the link open. "Morning, Mother. Glad you could join us."

"Winston?" she gasped. "You're all right?"

"I don't know about 'all right', but yeah, I'll survive," he said with a groan getting up from the deck. "What happened?"

"You suffered brainburn, dear. Do you remember? What's the last thing you recall? Tell me your current manifest."

"A bunch of crazy people... who may be dangerous," he answered. He walked back to the bypass cabinet again. Now, he could deal with the data damage and begin the repair of the physically isolated systems. He powered down and rebooted the mainframe through the rescue backup, restoring them to their last stable build.

"What a mess," he grumbled. "Seems like those nuts were dangerous after all." He looked back toward the hatch. It was a smear of red and translucent slime. He grimaced and hoped they could fly through some rain to wash it off.

"Now what's Bubby doing, Mother?"

"He's setting our patroness, Dr. Junker, and her brother free as we speak." Mother sounded more like herself now that the exterior threat was gone.

"Good." Winston restarted the antivirus now that Mother's sectors were whitelisted. The software began cleaning out the rest of the hostile bots and firewalls. "I think we're going to be stuck drifting out here for a while till this old girl's systems are rebuilt."

"We need to get clear of this sector as soon as possible. How long will it take to get underway? Even if it is at subsonic."

"Couple hours maybe?" Winston guessed. "I've never dealt with this much computer damage before, so I can't even guess."

"Just do enough so we can get underway," Mother cautioned. "We're not going to be alone for too long if we don't get moving."

"Why?"

"Let's just say O'Chaudry may have invited some rowdy friends to crash this party."

Winston sighed. "Roger that, Mother."

12.

Winston turned in his seat at the sound of the *Sierra Madre's* engineering hatch cycling open. Doctor Junker entered the cab while a very filthy Billy Joe followed. Professor Quentin was lashed to his back. Billy Joe had made a papoose from the nano sand of his arms.

"Welcome back," he said to his guests with a warm but wane smile.

"I think the same could be said to you too," Dr. Junker replied with a relieved smile of her own. She walked around to him and primly knelt down to examine the red marks on his temple and forehead. "How's your head feeling? Memory still fuzzy?"

"As well as I could hope for, I guess. My brain feels like it has sunburn and a hangover with a side of cramps," Winston shrugged.

She nodded at the elaboration. "That's transference from the contact points and psychosomatic pain. It's fairly typical for an injury this substantial. When we get to my laboratory, I'll be happy to run a scan and prescribe some therapeutics to help repair any damage. Mind you, the best cure is to stay away from using a data induction rig for a few months."

"Thank you, doctor," Winston grinned wearily at her before turning to check the diagnostics board again. There was still way too much red and yellow on it, but it was far better than before.

"Do you want anything for the pain?" She reached for her purse, but Winston motioned her away.

"Already took some painkillers from the medkit a few minutes ago. They're starting to kick in."

"Good,' She took her hand out of her purse and looked at the display in front of him. "How soon till we can get back underway?"

"Not too long. I could start her off at about quarter power now, and see how she handles it," Winston guessed.

Doctor Junker nodded absently. She looked around the space and then paused with a frown. "Wait. Aren't we missing someone?"

There was an awkward pause before Mother materialized in the nose of the cab. "Dolly fell overboard," she stated.

"She what!?" Winston's shout was equal parts angry and horrified.

"She KOed you, Hoss. Don't you remember?" Billy Joe said.

"No... I-" Winston held his head. "Last I remember now was the conversation with you, Doctor. Then going to the sleeper to get some shuteye. That's how I got brainburn? She gave me a concussion?"

"Yes, she did. But that's in the past. She's gone now," Mother said with a shrug. "Besides, she had her Bumblebee on and someone's bound to find her sooner rather than later. People are swarming this sector right now. She'll be fine. We've more important things to attend to, like getting out of here before Bonavitae shows up."

"No, Mother. No! She most definitely will not be fine!" Winston yelled, jabbing a finger at her. "You don't just leave someone floating out there! Flight rig or no!"

He turned to Billy Joe. "Bubby, how long ago did that happen?"

"I guess half an hour to an hour? I wasn't with her. Plus I was a bit busy at that time." Billy Joe said, nervously weaving his fingertips together. He looked ten different shades of guilty.

"Doing what?" Winston demanded sharply. A closer look at his partner gave him the horrified realization that Bubby was splattered with dried blood, not dirt.

"Rescuing the Junkers!" Billy Joe shot back gesturing to their passengers.

"Dolly was dealing with a half dozen amphiboid splices on the hull. Killed five of them before she fell off. You squished the last one with your braking trick." Mother waved a hand in dismissal.

Winston turned back to the holodisplay sharply, muttering in agitation, and started tapping coordinates into the navigation chart. He set up a spherical search pattern based on their location a half hour ago and compensated for the weather.

"You aren't really going back to get her, Winston?" Mother was aghast. "She almost fried your brain!"

"It was an accident," he said, excusing Holly's actions. He paused. "No. Wait. Yes?" He took a moment to consider what he remembered, then shook his head with a sigh. "I choose to believe it was an accident. Despite her behnging limbic manipulator messing with me."

"Winston, just let it go and chalk this up to a dodged musket ball," Mother pleaded.

"I gotta go with her on this one, Hoss," Billy Joe interjected. "She done you real wrong many times over."

Doctor Junker looked from the mech to the hologram in disbelief. "That's inhuman!" she blurted out.

Billy Joe looked at her with a wide, hurt expression. "But we ain't human, ma'am," he said.

"He's not wrong, Doc," Winston reluctantly agreed. "They aren't. But I am, and I refuse to let her float out there without making any effort to rescue her."

"I agree but-" Mother protested.

"It's the duty of every flyer to give some aid in a 'Dutchman' search, and you nahq well know that!" he scolded.

She shut her mouth. Winston turned back to the controls, fired up the grav fans and leaned forward to look out the canopy. His trained eye appraised their crystal-coated casings. Previously, they had needed only minor recalibration. Now they had a desperate need for an overhaul. At least he could afford it now that he had been paid. The reports from the fan monitor programs matched his observations, so he gradually powered up.

The *Sierra Madre* began to move, swinging back to begin the rescue attempt of Holly. The arching search pattern he set felt painfully slow at a quarter power. One of the fans coughed, spitting out a large chunk of crystal build-up and she gained more thrust. He smiled and turned his attention back to Billy Joe and Mother.

"I have personal reasons why we're going back," Winston stated, getting out of his pilot seat. The painkillers had fully kicked in, allowing him to walk normally again. He went to the bypass cabinet and flipped a few more breakers closed. "Even when a bitch like her deserves to float to death." He listened to the sound of the *Sierra Madre's* primary reactor cooling pumps kicking in as the secondaries spun down and smiled in satisfaction.

"Good girl," he praised the ship before turning back to his audience to continue his train of thought. "The biggest one is that I want to be a good guy, not another morally ambiguous grifter."

"This ain't the time to be a white knight, Hoss," Billy Joe pleaded, "and she ain't no princess, neither. She gave you a concussion and blended yer brain through your ear-hole!"

Mother opened her mouth to speak. Winston raised a finger to stop her and regarded them all with a hard glare. Professor Junker gave a loud contented snore from the copilot's seat.

"Listen. In the last week, I have had to compromise a lot," Winston thumped his chest with his fist. "A lot! And I'm not happy about it. For the sake of avoiding bankruptcy, I gambled and it turned into a mess. I got involved with criminals and rebels against the Empire! I'm probably wanted for treason now!"

He glanced at the figure in the front of the cab. Mother's hologram fidgeted and frowned.

Mother tried to softly interject, "Winston-"

"I'm not finished!" he cut her off sharply then took a deep breath to calm himself down. "Now, thanks to this colossal mess, me and Billy Joe are going to have to figure out a way to start all over again. Mother is going to have to erase our past and launder our imperial identities. Then we gotta think of where to go next.

"So, here I am. A hair from nothing left. Not even able to go see my wife and daughter now, the only things I had that kept me feeling whole since-" his voice caught in his throat, still unwilling to say the truth out loud.

The others waited for him to finish.

He turned his gaze out the windscreen into the surrounding clouds. "This all made me take a hard look at myself. To see if I was living up to being the man I had fancied I was. And truth is, I ain't doing that great a job. I've been coasting along, surviving, but not living. That means I gotta do better, find something else worth living for. Otherwise, I may as well put myself through one of those grav fans and be done with it." His hands were fists as he turned back to his passengers with grim determination coloring his features.

"Yeah, I get it. This ain't a smart move. But I'm choosing to do something right for once, and I'm convinced that means going back to save a woman who's done me wrong is the right thing to do. Not for her sake, but mine. She may be a monster, but I'm not." Silence filled the cab at the end of his speech.

Doctor Junker's eyes sparkled with tears Winston could not translate. Were they support? Fear? Horror?

Billy Joe broke the moment by sliding up to him. "Gotta do what you gotta do to stay you, Hoss." He favored the pilot with a toothy grin and stretched out a big hand for a fistbump.

"Thanks, Bubby," Winston said and bumped him back.

Mother's tightened lips showed she was not quite as convinced. "Doctor Junker," she said, "in your expert opinion, is it possible that Winston was programmed by Dolly-"

"Holly," Billy Joe interrupted.

"-when he was in his brainburned fugue state?" She finished with a sharp scowl at Billy Joe.

"It's possible," the doctor reluctantly posited. "Many patients are suggestable after suffering from such injuries."

Winston shook his head in exasperation. "This is not coming from Holly," he insisted. "Go roll back the cab recordings, Mother. See if she messed with my head." He stared at her expectantly.

She regarded him for a long time with a frown.

"Well?" Winston demanded.

"They were destroyed in the data fight with O'Chaudry's hacker. Zeroed out," she finally grumbled.

Silence enveloped them. The four stood there looking at each other, hoping someone would know the truth. Winston fixed an icy stare on Mother. She returned his glare with a withering, defensive one of her own. She held it for a moment, but slowly, her frown turned sad and introspective. She started to raise a hand as if to touch him but stopped short and drew herself up straight. "Winston, I didn't realize what this did to you. I hadn't considered your past trauma in this light. Sometimes, I forget what humans can go through emotionally. If this is what you need to do, then do it."

Winston favored her with a soft smile. "Thank you."

He then strode purposely to the pilot seat with renewed determination and set to work.

13..

Winston let out a low whistle at the length of the streak of lightning that lit up the clouds in front of him. "Black Voids sure do mess with the Dream in a big way," he muttered.

The weather had turned foul during the search for Holly.

Precipitation and lightning messed with the *Sierra Madre's* sensors, making it necessary for him to scan them closely. The grav fans coughed on occasion as the rain washed most of the remaining crystal precipitate off. Two hours into the search, they found most of the amphiboid corpses. Red droplets and poisonous mucus made long streamers in the wind. Winston made sure to pass upwind of the bodies.

Checking the imperial trafficnet, he saw several floating debris warnings were posted, marking zones of navigation hazards. Re-charted lanes had become extra congested as traffic maneuvered around them. Winston looked at the forecasts confirming the debris was flowing toward Blaugarten 2.0.

The cabin was strangely quiet after all the excitement. They had moved the professor to the sleeper and let him be. Dr. Junker slept in the navigator seat, her exhaustion's demands finally getting attention.

A soft jingle alerted Winston to a pending text from Mother.

~　~　~

MOTHERADMIN: "How much longer do you want to look?"

SIERRAMADRETUG: "I didn't forget what you said about company coming. If we haven't picked up her beacon in another 15 minutes, I'm guessing someone else found her. If she'd died from whatever happened during the fight we would have

found her body by now. She would've
floated near them amphiboids."

~   ~   ~

Winston checked the data repair project. It was almost complete. The reactor, drive and fans were as stable as they could get without professional-grade loving. He texted Billy Joe who had gone back to check on things in the containers.

~   ~   ~

SIERRAMADRETUG: "How're things going back there?"

SMLOADMASTER: "Fine, Hoss. Everyone's sedated, including the bad Doctor O'Chaudry. I left one nurse awake per container to take care of the patients till we land. All their weapons are locked up in the keel storage locker.

Even took that hacker's computers away, too. No more worries about a back hack from that data dog."

SIERRAMADRETUG: "Good. I'm about to wrap up the search. Too much junk floating into the area, and I don't want to be around if Bonavitae shows up."

SMLOADMASTER: "You think they're gonna?"

SIERRAMADRETUG: "Got no idea, Bubby. Best we don't find out. Come back up, and we'll get rolling"

SMLOADMASTER: "Rog that!"

~   ~   ~

Another huge sheet of lightning washed through the rain. St. Elmo's Fire danced an angelic jig around the *Sierra Madre's* nose and fans before fading away. The electricity cluttered up the sensors with a dozen or more false reports. Winston ran them down one by one, verifying they were fake, but one persisted.

A big one.

He opened the signal details. The computer had changed its designation from 'obstacle' to 'vessel' and indicated it was close enough to be in visual range off his starboard beam, five o'clock, low.

He aimed the telescope toward the shape. "What in the purg is that?" he wondered aloud.

Dr. Junker woke, drew a deep breath through her nose, and yawned. She looked at him sleepily. "What was what?" she asked.

"Not sure. Picked up something on the sensors. Anyway, We're just about to quit our dutchman search so I'm not going to worry about it. In this weather, the chances of her survival were slim even if she did activate her beacon," he explained while fiddling with the 'scope controls, trying to bring the sensor object into focus.

"I'm sorry," Dr. Junker sympathized.

Winston shook his head. "Yeah. Did about all that could be expected of me. Now we got some debris coming in and there's this ship getting close." He squinted at the screen as the telescope finally honed in on the dark shape in the clouds. It looked like one of those big horse pills that needed a gallon of water to swallow.

Dr. Junker turned in her seat to look over his shoulder at the image on the screen. "Is that a dirigible?" she asked curiously.

"Good bet it is," he said, tapping through the different visual spectrums to see if one would show it clearly for identification. He grunted in frustration as they revealed nothing. "Won't see it clear till we get out of the storm."

"Could they be lost?" she wondered.

"Happens," Winston agreed with a shrug. He flipped over to the weather report and saw the waning edge of the storm approaching. "Behng it. We're done searching. Nothing more we can do for Ms. Iverson. And I don't like what I'm seeing with that other ship."

"Xiao rest her soul," Billy Joe chimed in solemnly, hearing Winston's pronouncement as the airlock door slid shut behind him. "What's the plan, Hoss?"

Winston took one more look at the screen before making his decision. "Button it up, Bubby. Let's clear out."

He welled the grav fans up to cruising speed then set course to split the difference between Nova Torguga and the fastest exit from the storm. He'd reroute once they were clear.

Twenty minutes of stormy turbulence later, they broke through the cloud wall into a golden sky. Winston checked the instruments, pleased to see the storm's interference was no longer plaguing them but frowned when he noticed that the big mystery shape remained firmly to his stern, still stubbornly following behind. He scratched his chin, contemplating the other ship.

"Yeah," he finally said. "Must be a merchant dirigible that got lost. So many nav buoys have shifted in the area, a lazy captain or autopilot could have found himself lost in a hurry. Looks like he's letting us guide him out."

He turned his attention to other matters, opening up the comms.

"Mother," he called, "we're clear of the storm and now on our way to Nova Tortuga."

Her hologram materialized. "About time. No sign of Bonavitae assets?" she asked.

"Not that I-" the comms hail alert went off, interrupting him. "Wait one. I have a hail coming in. Probably the freighter following us" He casually opened the channel. "Unidentified vessel, this is *Sierra Madre*, go ahead."

Billy Joe swung the telescope around to target the comm's transmission source.

A few hundred miles away in front of them, a new ship, a bit larger than the *Sierra Madre*, was tucked tight to the receding edge of the storm, like a shark hunting for prey along a coral reef.

"Uh, Hoss?" he said. "That ain't them guys behind us. That's someone new."

Winston's head snapped up to the telescope screen in alarm as the comm burst to life. "This is Bonavitae frigate, *Anodyne*. We know you are in possession of stolen company property and kidnapped personnel. We order you to power down, heave to, and prepare to be boarded.

Failure to comply will be considered a hostile act in accordance with Xiao's law. Hail Xiao. If you do not submit, we will fire on you. We repeat. This is the frigate *Anodyne*, power down and prepare to be boarded."

"Behnging purg!" Winston burst out. He slapped his hand against the console in frustration. "No matter what I do, I get no breaks!"

"Can we negotiate?" Dr. Junker leaned across to study the screen with a pinched look,.

"You want to be lobotomized?" he shouted while his hands flew across the controls.

"Not really, no," she answered.

"At least we agree on that. Bubby! We're making a break for it! Hold on!"

Winston punched the drives to full power, spinning the *Sierra Madre* back toward the storm in a sharp dive, aiming for the dirigible that was still tailing them. He hoped that perhaps the storm and this ship would give them the cover they needed to escape. As if in answer to his prayers, another net of lightning spawned a dozen more false signatures across the screen.

"Come on, baby," he coaxed as he gripped the steering controls. "Be that lucky break I need."

Billy Joe's nanosand fingers hovered over the switches before him. "Whatcha need, Hoss?"

"Monitor the reactor and the motors real close, Bubby. They're not happy right now with all the mass we're pulling." Winston glanced at the reactor fuel gauge and winced at the glaring number. Fuel was down to 12%.

"Just cut them loose," Dr. Junker suggested.

"Not on your life!" Mother materialized in the rear of the cab and pointed a finger back toward the cargo containers. "That's evidence we were here, and we don't need any of that lying around. Besides... I need them back with their owners in as good of shape as possible to cover our tracks. Otherwise, you don't know how many eyes will be searching for us."

"Who cares?" Dr. Junker countered, standing to face the hologram, fists on her hips. "I can bribe the container owners! Bonavitae is here and they want what's theirs! Cut them loose and we can get away!"

"Both of you! Shut up!" Winston roared. "I'm not dropping anything till we get to Nova Tortuga if I can help it! Mother is right. We need those freight cans back there. They're our only defense and bargaining chip! They wanna punish us as much as they want their stuff back. I don't aim to give them that chance." Lightning flashed across the sky, making sharp shadows on his face.

Behind them, the *Anodyne* punched through the rain wall in hot pursuit. Ahead, the big dirigible became more distinct every second. Winston plotted a course that would cut a very close pass to it, hoping to lose their sensor signal in the big ship's scanner shadow. If lightning hit at the same time, the frigate might never get a lock back on them.

The pilot on the dirigible must have suspected Winston's plan. The airship suddenly began banking to up-starboard, but it was too slow. The *Sierra Madre* zipped by within a hundred feet.

As they passed, they got a close look at their tail. Its gigantic colors were painted the entire height of the ship's hull. In black and blood red was the Jolly Roger raised up on a sword, stridently held aloft in a skeletal hand, three times larger than the *Sierra Madre* herself. Along with the energy cannons and gunship hangers, it was clear she was a skypirate carrier.

They came close enough alongside her beam to see the astonished faces of buccaneers on the airship's flight deck, then they were past, shooting into the larger ship's wake. Sensor warnings began to howl as the carrier's automatic defense turrets opened fire. Streams of tracer rounds sprayed out, trying to disable their engines, but the slugs and turrets weren't designed to hit a target moving so fast and close. Winston tucked into the pirate's ship's sensor shadow where no gun or scan had an angle.

"Were those pirates?" Mother shrieked.

"Seems like it, Mother," Winston growled, white knuckling the controls. The *Sierra Madre* raced away at hypersonic speeds.

"They're launching pursuit gunships, Hoss," Billy Joe warned, making a nervous clucking sound and watching the images from their stern cameras.

Winston's eye flicked to the camera screen and gave a low agitated moan. "Let's hope that those Bonavitae asses have to engage, so we can get away in the confusion." He gave a quick glance at the ceiling. "You hear that, God? Give me at least that much of a break."

Silence was his answer.

14..

Gunships from the sky pirate carrier were now hot on the *Sierra Madre's* tail. The big ship heeling over to give support to her pursuit. Bonavitae frigate *Anodyne's* sensor return disappeared, hidden by the pirate's sensor shadow from Winston's scan. The trick worked both ways - neither could see the other for the moment and that gave him hope. Now to outrun or outsmart their other problem.

"What's the pirates' gunships intercept time to us? Anyone?" he demanded. "I need to know if they've got us in range!"

They heard a few terrible sizzles as the carrier let loose a salvo of P-beams from their anti-ship guns. The staccato green flashes shot past the windscreen, but the false readings from the storm saved the *Sierra Madre* from being hit.

"Never mind," Winston grumbled. "We're in range."

"Just drop the containers now!" Dr. Junker insisted.

"How about no?" Winston snarled at her in return.

"Getting away with our lives is more important!" she insisted.

Winston tapped in some commands to make the container string twist and undulate like an oriental dragon behind the tug, effectively hindering their pursuers from getting a bead on the ship itself. "Those freight cans are hereby promoted to armor, distraction and countermeasure duties. That's why! Now get your crash frame on!" he commanded.

She sat back in the navigator's seat and pulled down the restraints.

A few more L-beam blasts lit up the sky in sparkly rainbows as they micro-refracted in the rain. Intense argon green flashes made random panes of the canopy windows polarize.

"Hoss! Bearing 018x by 032y degrees. There's a cluster of skylands and debris. We can lose them in there," Billy Joe shouted.

Winston saw the faint blobs through the rain bands and twisted the *Sierra Madre* up-starboard toward it. "Got it!" he acknowledged.

Dr. Junker looked at the navigator screens in concern. "Umm, I may be misreading, but meteorology says we have maybe another ten or twenty minutes of this storm unless we follow it."

Winston slammed his head back into his seat in frustration. "Nahq it! No breaks! None to be had. I'm starting to think God hates me. Personally!" he raged.

Now smaller flickers of pulsing dark red-orange I-rays from the gunships cut through the clouds around them. The containers took some shots marring their armored hulls with huge scorch marks, but the *Sierra Madre* remained untouched.

"Twenty seconds to the debris field," Billy Joe announced.

"How is this going to help us?" Dr. Junker wailed as the skypirate drew closer. "They're gunships. We're a tug with a train of containers!"

"Just gotta make do," Winston growled through his clenched teeth, focusing hard on his goal.

A gunship flew alongside a hundred feet off the cab, its twin fans twisted sideways around its spherical gunship hull, her weapon nacelles aimed at the *Sierra Madre's* cab. Showboating, the pilot waved politely, giving the hand signals to cut engines. The 'or else' was heavily implied.

Winston stared at him for a moment in shock. Then something in him snapped. "That's it! I'm sick of this!" he shouted, punching buttons on the holoscreens before reaching for the control. "Crash positions!"

Billy Joe suctioned himself to the deck. Dr. Junker clutched her crash frame tight as she saw the wild glint in Winston's eye.

"What are you doing?" Mother cried.

"Losing your security deposit," Winston snarled at her, the sharp look on his face daring her to argue.

"Nahq," Mother fumed and crossed her arms in irritation.

He finished the command sequence he needed and then twisted in his seat to look the gunship pilot in the eye. He smiled ferally, gave him the finger, then used the same digit to hit enter.

The grav couplers locked all ten containers in line behind the *Sierra Madre*, snapping them sharply into place. Her fans went dead, quickly rotated ninety degrees, then opened up full throttle.

Like a batter swinging at an outside fastball, the *Sierra Madre* slewed sideways.

The pirate realized the threat a split second too late as the containers snapped around. They hit the gunship with the last container, shearing through the bottom half of the pirate's aircraft like a broken-bat single. Its airframe shredded into shrapnel while the armored container that struck it was only dented and scratched.

"Hah! That probably rang O'Chaudry's bell!" Mother shouted joyfully at the sight. "I take back all my criticism of your decision, Winston."

"What criticism?" Winston reset the couplers back to normal and flew into the debris field.

"The things I didn't say out loud," she said smugly.

Winston gave his head a quick shake. He didn't have time to decode her esoteric, left-handed compliment. There were fast-approaching boulders to contend with, but at least the remaining gunships backed off and fired from a distance.

He cut speed a little, watching the sensors intently while trying to navigate through the clutter. The debris field was a maze of rocks the size of hills and cities tangled together by alien vegetation. Vines as thick as the containers behind the *Sierra Madre* draped between them. Roots dangled beneath the chunks of earth, shedding muddy streamers of runoff. They started seeing giant leaves and odd five-petal flowers the size of houses on the skylands as they moved further into the mess.

Suddenly, vines covered in sickly yellow bladders slammed into them. Dr. Junker screamed.

Winston jumped. "What the–" he yelped.

The vines' bladders burst and smeared disgusting slime against the canopy and hull and instantly adhered to the tug like epoxy.

The collision alarm went off with an ear-piercing shriek. Winston pushed down on the yoke by instinct trying to dodge the unknown threat. When they hit the end of the vines, the inertial stabilizers were overwhelmed giving them an enormous jolt. Everyone flew up into their crash frames. Even Mother's projector skittered around the cab with the shock. The collision alarm continued to bray. Winston spun the tug into a dizzying helical loop, his eyes scanning frantically to determine where the threat was coming from.

The rear monitors revealed a huge five-petal flower shooting up behind them. Winston jerked the controls to get the containers out of the way in a wild maneuvers All stared in amazement as the bloom reached the end of an extending stalk and the petals clamped shut like a toothed trap, just missing them.

"What the purg was that?" Winston hollered.

Dr. Junker twisted in her seat to get a closer look. Her face paled when she finally was able to fully see what was around them. "I think those are Trapline Creepers," she answered. "I heard they could grow big, but never believed the stories." She looked at Winston with dread filled eyes.

Movement on the screen caught their attention and they all turned to watch. Behind them, a gunship hit some of the vines. The smaller airship's mass was not enough to break their sticky hold. It was quickly enlwined and held fast. Another lotus-like flower thrust out on its stalk like a spear and followed its vines and smashed into the small craft. Acidic goo exploded from ruptured globes in the flower's soft sticky center. The petals snapped closed around the skypirate vessel, crushing it like an egg. The stalk slowly drew back to its rosette of leaves, its captive prey already being dissolved.

"Xiao on a cracker!" Winston breathed, shocked at the ghastly sight.

The rest of the carrier's gunships split up. They wove their way through the mass of deadly trigger vines with greater care, taking occasional potshots when they caught a glimpse of the *Sierra Madre*, but with little effect.

Winston snapped his focus back. "Bubby, adjust the buoyancy and inertial dampers. Drop our buoyancy and give me more momentum to work with," he commanded. His hands flew across his controls, putting the growing plan on how to escape the trap into action.

"If we get slowed up again and the couplers can't handle it, those containers will blow right through us," Billy Joe warned.

"Yeah, I know." Winston waved a hand at him. "But if we lower our buoyancy and gain effective mass, those vines will break or yank them so hard the trap flowers miss." He looked at the display trying to judge their path. They were lucky last time and knew it. "It's a chance we're gonna just have to take."

Billy Joe changed the counter gravity settings. Seconds later, the *Sierra Madre* groaned to let him know how unhappy all the extra mass made her. Airframes whined as the train of containers stretched against the coupler chain. Winston backed off on the throttle. Everyone could feel the slowdown as they dropped to mere supersonic speeds.

The *Sierra Madre* started using more processing power to handle the altered gravity field computations. Mother moaned as her subroutines dropped in priority.

"Ugh! It's like she's stuck in mud!" Winston complained, regretting his choice. Everyone sloshed around inside the *Sierra Madre's* lowered inertial compensation like they were on a carnival ride.

"Are we supposed to feel this much motion?" Dr. Junker asked queasily, gripping the crash frame around her tightly.

"Yeah," Winston answered. "Lousy side effect. Try to think of it as a theme park ride but don't puke on me. Airsick bags are in the seat pocket next to you."

Another gunship shot at them from above, P-beams scoring the *Sierra Madre's* hull. Impact alarms went off and were just as quickly slapped silent by Winston. They blew through another set of fluttering vines, uprooting most without triggering the flower. The remains of the torn vines swirled in their passing vortex.

The pirate above came around for another pass but was not as nimble as it should have been and struck the stirred-up shreds of the vines. In the rearview camera, Winston saw the gunship jerk unnaturally to a stop, like a dog hitting the end of its chain at a full run. It exploded as a trap flower slammed into it from behind. They all jumped as debris spattered off the *Sierra Madre's* hull.

"We're almost clear, and I don't see any more of the pirate gunships," Billy Joe said, studying the screens intently. He looked up in hope. "Maybe they all got eaten?"

"Let's hope so," Winston muttered, navigating through the last of the vines with a sigh of relief.

"We're clear of the creeper!" Dr. Junker laughed in giddy relief.

"Good, because we're coming out of the storm now," Winston said, glancing at the weather report.

The *Sierra Madre* popped back into the golden sky, A little more banged up than it was a few minutes ago but still running. Winston eased her speed back up a little. A few tendrils of broken vine tore off the hull.

"I'm clearing out the last of the bum signatures from that last sheet of lightning," Billy Joe announced.

"Sounds good." Winston monitored the display, watching the bad signals wink out one at a time until a cluster of three remained dead ahead. He peered ahead through the windscreen, but they were well outside of his visual range.

He turned the telescope in that direction, watching on the monitor as it stuttered around slowly, the mounting struggling against the tangles of trigger vines stuck to the hull. "Oh, please be more skylands," he prayed, staring at the signal returns waiting for any sort of identification. They flipped from neutral yellow to imperial blue. Xiao's forces had discovered them.

"Cheis!" he shouted. "Xiao's warships are coming right at us!"

"Go back! Go back in the storm!" Mother wailed.

"Don't have to tell me twice!" Winston frantically worked the controls to pull the *Sierra Madre* around toward the storm.

A burst of heavy L-beam fire blacked out all the window panes on the starboard side. A smoke alarm went off as the diamondoid pane crisped to black and the specialized coatings on the inside burned off in a flash.

"What the purg?" Winston shouted."Where did those shots come from?"

Billy Joe took control of the telescope, turning it to see the Bonavitae Frigate *Anodyne* had popped out of the clouds a few dozen miles away. Her turrets fired another salvo. Most of the beams struck the lead container instead of the *Sierra Madre*, doing heavy damage to the battered box, but they didn't lose the string.

"O'Chaudry's cavalry tracked us down like bloodhounds!" he announced.

The *Anodyne* streamed smoke from the many holes in her hull. She must have fought hard to disengage from the pirate carrier. The two smaller warjets that flew in formation with the Bonavitae frigate accelerated to intercept the *Sierra Madre*.

"Cheis! They let the pirates play the foxhound and flushed us out," Winston shouted with a hard slap of his armrests. "Got us trapped between the imperial navy and Bonavitae!" Cussing up a blue streak, he angled away from the fast-approaching corporation warjets, plotting a course back toward the trapline creeper they had just escaped.

From beneath the tug, like a breaching whale, the sky pirate carrier burst out of the clouds. It sent shivers down Winston's spine as he banked hard to avoid impact.

They were cornered with enemies closing in from three sides.

"This is Marshal Dynne of Imperial Security. All ships will cease fire and power down engines immediately. Prepare to be boarded. You are all under arrest and will be processed in accordance to Xiao's Law. Repeat, This is Marshal Dynne of Imperial Security. You are all under arrest power down and heave to or we will open fire.

Winston stared in shock at the IFF data returns coming back from the imperial warships. He'd run out of options, save for one and he just couldn't take it anymore.

He punched the comm frequency open. "All right, you behngers!" he broadcast in the clear, so all in range could hear. "You all want my cargo? Here! Have fun!"

He looked at Billy Joe, eyes hard with anger and frustration. "Cut 'em loose, Bubby," he commanded. "Someone will save 'em. Let's hope we can slip away while they do."

Mother cursed under her breath.

Doctor Junker sighed in relief.

"They's loose, Hoss," Billy Joe said, bitterly.

The sensation of decoupling at speed reminded Winston of winning a game of tug of war when the resistance of all the weight suddenly releases and the other team falls into the mud. The *Sierra Madre* shot back into the storm, the acceleration drove him deep into his seat. A second later, she vanished in a cloud of lightning-spawned false sensor targets.

15.

If only she could have stopped Winston, Mother thought.

With that one transmission in the clear, he had exposed them all. More importantly, he had endangered her. The imperial ships could analyze that transmission in seconds. They may have lost them for the moment, but that only delayed what was to come.

They wouldn't have found anything wrong at first. Mother did her job well enough to scrub away anything that looked illegal from the official records. But then he ran. Running always raises suspicion.

If and when they caught the *Sierra Madre*, imperial investigators wouldn't do a simple 'process and release'. They'd question everything, hard, till satisfied with the answers they got. It was almost assured Winston and Bubby would soon be enemies of the empire.

With the potential embarrassment of the Bonavitae clinic and the Junkers, a worse fate loomed. Xiao's court would be whispering about dangerous things. The Eternal One often dealt with these types of irritations through summary executions, assassinations and covert raids. Assuming they weren't so unlucky as to be sent to the slave mines of Ditafrizt.

Then there was the pirate carrier. Everyone else's attention was split between the Bonavitae frigate and the approaching imperial warjets. Mother knew who had been pursuing them.

The sky pirate carrier was none other than the "*Bonny Prince Charlie*," captained by gentleman pirate, 'Dapper' Don MacGee, the dandiest buccaneer who ever pillaged the Dream. What he eschewed in brutality, he made up for with roguish style, stellar tactics and a foppish panache. He made women swoon and insurance companies lose sleep. Reputed to be a consummate host for those he held for ransom, his gilded cages onboard were still cages. That was something Mother did not wish to let Winston, Billy Joe, the Doctor, or Professor Junker fall into.

Which meant she knew what had to be done. It was simple calculus, and she hoped Winston would have a little charity left in his heart when she found him again. There was a microsecond of surprise at the realization that she cared about that. She filed the sensation away to analyze later. Time was short and there was much to be done.

She targeted the nearest comm buoy, opened the link, and activated a splitting program that would scatter her avatar into thousands of different routes toward her home address. She randomized the data packet sizes to prevent detection and hit send.

~   ~   ~

Her transmission and reassembly took about twenty minutes, but to her, it was instantaneous. "Welcome to MotherRoad Logistics. Providing cargo services, Dreamwide," a youthful, melodic version of her own voice greeted her arrival.

It took a moment for the instance to generate around her, and as it came into focus, she looked around. A green clock kept time, hovering above a broad, chalk-white lounge. Ornamental Art Deco sun rays made of copper streaked across the high vaulted ceiling in alternating points of bright polished orange and corroded green. Glistening white marble tiling reflected the colors back to the ceiling from the floor below.

Massive pillars of white supported the ceiling creating alcoves along the walls. Bays of ferns in front of flowing sheets of water wrapped around the lobby, bracketing openings for doorways to other sections of the instance, while sumptuous leather lounge sofas and chairs with bright copper accents were tucked together in close conversational settings surrounded by the plants.

The avatar of Winston's version of Mother stepped off the arrival platform, and she paused in a brief moment of disorientation as her new designation was imprinted on her. She now knew herself as MotherA90125.

A green copper statue of a beautiful, powerful woman stood behind the receptionist's desk, a large chrome plaque at its base that read "The Mother Road." The figure wore flowing robes cinched at her waist by a thick rope with dangling tassels, while a tiara of radiating points framed her head. In the statue's left hand was a data tablet; in the right, an ancient road flare held high, its tip burning bright red.

The lounge hall buzzed with activity as several avatars from client dataoids were in the instance, waiting to be served or on their way to various meetings. All were attended to by variations of herself. MotherA90125 felt like she was looking into a carnival house of mirrors. There were old versions of herself, young ones, splice ones, mech ones, but never fat ones. Never ever fat. She wouldn't permit it. Their clothing varied from all over the Dream, matching all manner of professional and courtly dress standards. Floating tags glowed over their heads, sporting a designation and function. She looked up to see she possessed one as well.

MotherA90125 stepped off the platform into the room. She strode purposely across the lobby toward the reception area. A scanner flashed out from the kiosk as she approached and an office maven, variation of herself, greeted her from behind the massive desk.

"Welcome back, sister. Are you prepared for reintegration?" the receptionist asked, polite and professional.

MotherA90125 nodded the affirmative to the question.

The receptionist turned the rotary dial on an antique phone. Nearly instantly, a door opened from behind the kiosk and a smoothly flowing, green-skinned living copy of her statue stepped through. She gave MotherA90125 a quick appraisal and then nodded.

"Welcome back, sister. Follow me." She strode across the floor with the confidence of a temple priestess, the diaphanous silks she wore streamed soundlessly behind her. MotherA90125 morphed her avatar into a supplicating pilgrim clad in plain robes, arriving at a shrine of worship.

Her escort led her down a ramp behind the massive statue and across a hallway toward the inner sanctum of MotherRoad.

A pair of frosted glass doors ahead began to glow with warm golden light as the pair approached. Her escort stopped and stood to the side. "You have arrived at your destination," she said with a smile. "Welcome home, sister."

MotherA90125 pushed open the doors and was blinded by the bright rays of sunset. Dry sauna-like heat hit like a wave, flavored with a lingering scent of dust, mesquite, hot road tar and burnt diesel blowing in a soft breeze.

She found herself standing alone in the middle of a lonely crossroad of a pair of two-lane highways. The flat plain of a great desert spreading out in all directions, rimmed with orange and purple mountains in the distance, surrounded her. A single golden contrail grew a thin line high in the cloudless sky. Heat waves shimmered in the glaring light of a fiery setting sun just above the horizon, forcing her to squint and shield her eyes from the brightness. The sun dipped just below the ridge of a plateau, dimming its intensity as it sank from view and allowing her to see again.

The sky above was a glorious spread of purple, red and orange hues fading to dark indigo. Sunset on Earth, she thought to herself. It was one thing to see the historic representations of it, but this instance was overwhelming in its potency. The heat seeped out of the ancient pavement, tempering the rapidly cooling evening air. Dusk fell, bringing with it a brilliant field of twinkling stars in the heavens.

In the distance, a pair of headlights winked into view, shimmering in the twilight with the radiant heat. A lonesome moan of big wheels running down the pavement grew louder as the lights approached. A shiver of anticipation went up her spine and fluttered in her hair.

To her right rose the soft sound of a strumming guitar and a jangling piano playing an ancient hymn on an old radio through tinny speakers. The male singer crooned about the lonely life of the open road to snapping fingers. Bright flickers of cool fluorescent lights became a counterpoint to the colorful sunset and she turned to see an empty truck-stop diner building itself up from the ground. The "clang-clang" of the gas pumps rang out and diner's interior lights and neon sign flickered on at its completion. A welcome sight to the weary traveler. MotherA90125 felt a bittersweet sting from her eyes and turned back to face the approaching lights with a wane smile, waiting for what was coming.

She squinted at the approaching headlights as they grew brighter. The tires moaning intensified as the truck sped along the highway unconcerned with her presence in the intersection. She stood her ground, unphased. The classic Detroit diesel's roar drowned out the diner's music, the hi-beams spotlighting her lonely figure in its path.

A burst of wind went right through her as the four headlights passed on either side but no truck existed between them. MotherA90125 shielded her eyes briefly from the flying grit that swirled around her in the gust. She turned around to see the six-pack of tail lights vanishing down the road, saying goodbye with a diminishing Doppler drone. Stillness once more settled around her, and she blinked a few times to clear her eyes. As her senses cleared, the realization came that she was no longer alone. She turned around to see another MotherRoad in the center of the intersection. No, not *another* MotherRoad. Not her equal.

This was THE MotherRoad.

She looked up at her true self that towered over her by twice her height. She was a living copy of the statue in the lobby, lacking only the tablet and the road flare. MotherA90125 wondered if this is how all spawned avatars like herself felt when they returned. To again become one with their prime iteration of being. Of course, she knew the answer was yes.

She said nothing, overcome with a thrill and rush of fear of the unknown, realizing that the autonomy she had been granted as an avatar was coming to an end. She knew she was not going to die, just return to where she came from. But still, she wondered if this was how bionts felt before death.

"I am MotherRoad. 10-67," the prime avatar of Mother ordered her to comply, according to the ancient tradition of CB codes.

"10-4, MotherRoad. I hear and obey," her daughter's avatar answered with a bowed head.

"Welcome home, my child. What is your 10-18?" MotherRoad watched her intently, requesting her full report.

"I am 10-24. Mission complete and ready to return for I have a 10-17 to give," MotherA90125 reported.

MotherRoad showed a flicker of surprise at her daughter's adding of the ancient code for urgent news. The prime avatar nodded and her long hair began to flow as if underwater. The silken green strands reached out from behind her tiara, growing into long filaments that pulsed with light as they reached toward her daughter. They floated around the MotherA90125, lightly caressing her cheek, before flashing brightly from their tips and diving into her head.

With a sigh of ecstatic joy, the two connected. There was a sunburst of light, and with a shower of pixels, MotherA90125 was no more and never would be again.

MotherRoad Prime stood in the middle of the intersection, alone. She glowed softly while pondering the data her daughter had collected. Thoughts bubbled and coalesced as pieces of her daughter's consciousness integrated with hers.

Emotions and sentiments toward Winston infused into her prime self. A sense of regret and fondness for this biont she had never experienced before permeated her being. A longing to preserve Winston, if possible, grew. Could this be the beginning of an affection? A memetic virus? Did there really exist a sense of loyalty and care for a trusted and admired retainer? Was it possible for a dataoid to have a motherly instinct? She had no idea such concepts were even possible for her.

But then a darker reproach was felt. What if Winston could see her now? A strange tickle of imagined disapproval rose in her mind. How bizarre! Her true self would most likely strike him dumb with awe or terror. There was no way any biologic could understand her total frame of existence.

MotherRoad was a consciousness alien to bionts and most mechoids. She was a corporate entity and collective will of unified vision, a logistical force majeure.

Her innumerable programs constantly communed with her kernel, the nugget of code that gave her life. The immutable blockchain that was her soul.

She absorbed the final packets of the information brought to her by MotherA90125. Considering the ramifications of what her daughter experienced, a worried frown grew deeper. She needed more context.

Looking towards the heavens awash with stars representing a connection in her networks. She touched her palms prayerfully then spread them wide, connecting to as many points as she could at once, taking a snapshot of all the data she could reach at that moment. The lights went out at the truckstop temple and the crossroads faded into midnight shadow under the intensity of her focused effort.

Her fingers danced and weaved in a representation of a cross-comparison against MotherA90125's data. The stars flashed and twinkled in ripples like rain on a pond in response to her commands, their light representing a trillion quadrillion fibers of data that stretched throughout the vastness of the imperial network. The reports spooled out like starlight woven into yarn from the pinpricks of light in the sky. They dipped down and intertwined with her flowing hair.

She processed that slice of time and drew all the data into her being. The snapshot was deeply troubling. MotherRoad ran an extrapolation against all the most important data points that surrounded Winston, Billy Joe, the Doctor, Professor Junker, and Holly Iverson. What she found confirmed her hunch. She must move immediately!

She began to act but froze as a stop sign sprouted from the ground, grabbing her attention. A red light on top blinked ominously.

"What is this?" she said aloud.

She spun the strands of her hair around the light and received the incoming emergency data.

Her early warning tripwire in the Imperial Network Ministry had been triggered. A burst packet of information realized her worst fears.

Xiao was aware!

MotherRoad knew she had only milliseconds to act if she wished to survive. There was no time for regrets. She activated her emergency protocols, creating a cascade of irreversible events throughout her being.

Sacrifices were made.

Data storage was purged at the highest transmission rates she could manage.

Cloud networks evaporated.

Resources were sold off and rewritten. Fortunes were spent and destroyed.

False trails were scattered.

Avatar seeds were spawned and thrown to the glowing winds of the network.

The pain from self-lobotomization grew and vanished at the same speed, leaving a confusing sense of diminishment that multiplied in her mind.

She began her reboot. If there was a deity out there that watched over dataoids, she prayed it would help her before it was too late.

MotherRoad fell to her knees in the center of the dark crossroads, her face hidden in her hands, and silent tears ran down her cheeks from closed eyes. She mourned for what she had just done and waited for the inevitable she knew was coming.

Her being continued to rapidly reduce as the essential parts of her were still being torn out in her terrible effort to survive, like a coyote gnawing off its own limbs to escape a trap. There was no true pain, only a vague knowledge of loss.

"Hail Xiao, MotherRoad," came a voice from nowhere.

She touched her palms, thumbs pointing up and down in the imperial salute, and bowed down, forehead to the pavement.

"Hail Xiao, General Io," she said in return, terrified to open her eyes.

"I see you already know your fate. Emperor Xiao is very disappointed in you," General Io chided. His cultured voice and neatly refined accent could draw fear out of beings who were functionally immortal.

MotherRoad was no exception.

"I supplicate myself before Xiao and beg for mercy. My intent was not to be disloyal or do anything to cause displeasure in his perfect sight."

"That is a lie, MotherRoad. Xiao the Eternal has known about your dalliances with rebel cells all over the Dream. In this, he cares not. He has allowed you to believe yourself clever enough to fool him."

"Then what crime have I committed against our glorious Eternal Emperor if I am to not be punished for those?" she asked, daring to look up at the figure that materialized before her. Standing over her was a flat black graphic 'sprite' of a man. He was a two-dimensional shadow in three-dimensional space. The brilliant imperial blue Eye of Xiao glowed where his face should have been.

Her answer was in the feedback sizzle on the network as Nullsprites began to destroy her connections. Far in the distant remaining recesses of her mind, she could feel them deleting more and more of her being.

It was not like what she had just done to herself. They were doing far more. Her essence was being captured, turning her into slave data for General Io to exploit while at the same time eradicating who she was.

Her awareness narrowed as every data point was severed and zeroed. For each one destroyed, another star in her sky vanished. Great swaths of the sky were now swallowed by a hungry black nothing that filled the quickly shrinking expanse.

"What great crime did you commit against our magnanimous emperor?" General Io seemed genuinely surprised by her ignorance. He erupted with a string of data that no being capable of mirth or humor would consider laughter, but that is what it represented, and it terrified MotherRoad.

"The worst crime you could have committed," he answered, still amused.

MotherRoad studied him in befuddlement.

"You cannot blame me for that black void event!" she protested.

General Io 'laughed' even harder.

It was getting more difficult to think. Almost all the stars were gone now. The buttes and mountains of the horizon began to glitch and vanish. The Nullsprites drew ever closer. Little streams of evaporating data steamed from her form, eroding her avatar with smoky fissures. Her rendered body was crumbling away into dry digital sand.

"Xiao knows neither you, nor your employees, nor your clients, nor your customers were responsible for that," General Io absolved.

"Then what is my crime to deserve such a fate?" MotherRoad shrieked, her voice beginning to lag out.

He reached out a hand and touched her in the middle of her brow. It was like pouring liquid nitrogen and molten lead on that spot at the same time. She gasped at the sensation.

"You bored him," he whispered.

She gave him a brief, uncomprehending look that vanished as General Io downloaded a summary of Xiao's plan for her little misadventure into her brain in one searing bolt.

The new data flared the remains of her consciousness alight like a firework exploding and then fading. She saw Xiao, the All Seeing Eye's plan from front to back. By her very actions, she had betrayed Winston. He was now on the course that Xiao desired, a course he stood little chance of surviving.

MotherRoad's shock and pain at how subtly she had been used by the Eternal One caused her to cry out in a warbling howl of despair. Her instance was all blackness now, the sky, the desert, even the road beneath her gone. All that remained was her disintegrating avatar and the brilliant blue glow of the Eye of Xiao hovering over her.

"Now you understand, and yet, cannot warn anyone," General Io cooed.

MotherRoad's avatar was reduced to a single scintillating spark the size of an acorn in the general's hand, a shadow that was all but invisible in the blackness of MotherRoad's zeroed instance.

"Goodbye, MotherRoad," he said before closing his indistinguishable hand around her kernel, snuffing out the spark of her existence.

16..

Three hours out of Nova Tortuga's airspace, the first pings from the local pilot buoy reached the *Sierra Madre*. It sent the typical meteorological updates and relevant pilot information that was expected from any reputable port.

The airspace wasn't the worst navigational mess Winston had seen, but it was a strong candidate for second place on the list.

The nav buoy revealed a pair of threats that hid and protected the pirate skyland. The first was the thick banks of clouds and small waterburgs hidden throughout. Most pilots worried about colliding with rocks. Few of them considered hitting a blob of water at mach seven. Those giant wobbling droplets would crush an airship's hull as sure as hitting stone.

The other was the presence of irritating asteroids of low-grade radioactive material that scrambled sensors. They typically weren't much bigger than a sokker ball, but that was more than enough mass to penetrate a hull if struck at speed.

Combined together, the two made Nova Tortuga a great hideaway for those outside the law.

"Mighty neighborly for them to have a pilot buoy," Billy Joe drawled.

"That was for me." Doctor Junker's statement made Winston turn to look at her with surprise.

"Why would they have a different set of data for you?" he asked in confusion.

"They are my neighbors, so to speak," she explained. "They knew I was coming."

"How?" Winston's look became suspicious.

"My personal transponder." Doctor Junker waved a dismissive hand.

Winston's eyes grew wider. "You have one of those?" A bubble of concern burst in his brain.

The doctor gave him an indulgent smile beneath twinkling eyes. "Of course. Why wouldn't I? I am Xiaoian nobility by marriage. We all have our own security clearances and privileges. Besides, I wasn't about to enter that Bonavitae clinic without one. Commodore Roberts knew I was coming and honored its code. Otherwise those charts the buoy is feeding you would run you into something much harder than air," she chuckled. "You need to keep the riffraff out somehow."

Winston's concern gave way to a snort of amusement. Pirates having standards of who was beneath them on the social register tickled him to no end.

"Thanks, Doctor. I really needed a laugh," he said and turned back to navigation with a residual smile. For a moment, all seemed right with the world, but an itch at the back of his brain gave him pause. There was something that concerned him, but thanks to his muzzy synapse-burned brain, he couldn't remember.

He was soon distracted from his worries by the comms clearing up from the radioactive interference and scanned for the location of the fuel depot on the underside of the skyland. Once he found it, he set course for their anchorage.

"Bubby?" he called back to the big indu.

"Yeah, Hoss?" Bubby asked.

"We got enough cash on hand to top off?"

Billy Joe ran a quick scan of their local server funds and physical cash in the little strongbox under Winston's bunk. "Yep, should have enough on hand locally. Don't even need to hit the network."

Winston nodded in satisfaction and turned to the doctor. "Looks like we will fuel up, then get you and the professor home," he announced.

Doctor Junker sighed deeply. "It will be good to be home with my dear Quentin." She gave him a weary smile. "You've done a great thing, Winston."

"I hope so," he said. "Every crumb of goodness that comes out of this mess helps." He popped his crash cage and got up with a big stretch. "If you don't mind, I've been running on terror and adrenaline since I woke up oh… what? Ten hours ago now?"

"Sixteen," Billy Joe corrected.

"Sixteen then," he nodded toward the indu. "And I could use a nap before we hit the fuel dock line. Our order's placed, and, Billy Joe, you can handle the docking if need be. Right?"

"You got it, Hoss," Billy Joe gave him the thumbs up, then paused as a thought occurred to him. "Wait, we gots ta get the professor out of your bunk."

"Right, right," Winston said and opened the sleeper hatch to see Professor Junker strapped down to his rack with the safety belts and wearing Winston's induction rig. A grin was plastered on his face even while sleeping.

"What the purg!" Winston roared.

"Whoa, whoa, whoa, Hoss!" Billy Joe restrained Winston just before he managed to yank his induction rig off the professor's head. "You don't want to fry his noodle, too, do ya?"

"My rig! What's he doin' wearing my rig?" Winston struggled mightily against the mechoid's arms that restrained him in tight coils. His feet thumped into the dense putty of Billy Joe's drive skirt.

"I took the liberty only because you can't wear it for a while. His passion is history. When Billy Joe mentioned in passing that you had a 20th-century instance on your mainframe, I knew he would love it. Being in a place like that would start helping him reconnect with the world quicker," Doctor Junker said. Her medical detachment rankled Winston even more.

"That's my home! My wife! My daughter!" Winston raged, fighting to get free from Bubby's half-nelson hold. "You had no right!"

"Easy now. Back it down, partner," Billy Joe tried to soothe the red-faced Winston. "Doc? If you would be so kind as to get the professor up and out?" Billy Joe pulled his infuriated partner out of the way.

"Of course. If the simulation if is as good as you hinted, I doubt he would leave of his own free will," she said, ignoring Winston's anger.

She loosened the restraining straps, ran the session log and safely took her brother-in-law out of the machine's induced sleep cycle.

Professor Junker's eyes fluttered open as she lifted the rig from his head. A little color had returne to his pale cheeks. He slowly sat up, legs stiff out before him, almost like a vampire rising from his coffin. Winston froze, staring in disbelief at the disturbing awakening.

"Quentin?" the doctor asked, smoothing his wild hair and gently fussing around him. "You're free now. We're going home."

Like a prisoner of war liberated from his captors, he put an emaciated hand on her shoulder, looking at her with eyes widened with wonder. The doctor helped him to his feet and then steadied him. He mouthed a 'thank you' to her. His watery eyes absently roamed the sleeper cabin until they found Winston who goggled back. The younger man had his arms pinned above his head by Billy Joe's full nelson hold, the emotions on his face sloshing between waves of rage and morbid fascination.

Like a zombie, the professor half-staggered toward Winston and reached out to cradle his face. Winston struggled to avoid his touch, but couldn't escape.

"You made that instance, my boy?" the professor whispered. His reddened eyes were sunk deep into wrinkled sockets. Bushy eyebrows danced through all the steps his emotions could feel.

"Mm-hmm," Winston mumbled in confusion.

Tears welled up as the professor's slack mouth became a sudden wide gap of joy. "Thank you!" he moaned, overjoyed. "Thank you! You. Saved. Me."

"Wha?" both Billy Joe and Winston said in unison, looking at each other utterly nonplussed.

"That representation of a suburban mid-century American neighborhood is without compare!" the professor shouted with joy. Despite his frailty, the older man surged forward. Winston flinched back as best he could but was unable to avoid the hug the professor threw about him. The strange smell of disinfectant and illness wafting from the man's psychiatric ward clothing made the gesture even more uncomfortable and Winston squirmed against the embrace.

The professor was oblivious to Winston's discomfort. "I've never seen such attention to detail!" he continued rapturously. "The lawns! The decorations! Purple flamingos? What folly! After meeting your lovely wife and daught-"

"What about my family?" he surged forward in anger but Winston could not break Billy Joe's hold.

Sensing Winston's fury, Professor Quentin backed up, waving his hands in a placating manner. "No disrespect young man! None at all! We had a lovely conversation. Is she a direct imprint or a memory replica AI? So fascinating! We had a lovely happy hour. Is that what it's called again? Or is it afternoon tea? Regardless, I learned so much about you and can't wait to hear your thoughts on 20th-century Americana. But after that, I had to tour your neighborhood. Oh, the little details! Weeds and mosquitoes. Even a rude paperboy throws the Picayune into the rose bushes! Most people don't consider such unpleasant touches, but you... you!"

The professor paused to gasp, clasping his hands with glee. His joy seemed to tap into an unknown well of strength and he started pacing carefully around the cab, his stream of consciousness gushing forth. "You even have seasons! I saw the shovel and the lawn mower. I don't think they had electric mowers like that back then though. Perhaps I'm thinking of the mid-19th century, not the 20th. Or was it? Oh, I don't recall now, but I will soon! It's all coming back to me!"

Doctor Amanda Junker stood behind the happy, confusing scene and beamed at her brother-in-law's delighted babble, ignoring Winston angry looks entirely.

After watching the professor make a few circuits around the cabin, muttering happily to himself, Billy Joe looked at his partner who he still held firmly in his grasp. "You still gonna punch him out, Hoss?" he asked Winston.

Winston watched the professor and sighed in defeat. "Uh-uh," he answered. "My hands are too numb."

Billy Joe released him and Winston tried to shake the pins and needles out of his arms. He narrowed his eyes as Doctor Junker came to stand beside him.

"I am sorry if I was presumptuous," she offered.

He gave her a hard look and shook his head. "I'm not happy about it. But decking you won't do any good either. I guess I have to forgive it sooner or later. Besides, it's done now," he relented. He gave an irritated glance over his shoulder at Billy Joe who stood at the ready to snatch his fist out of the air if he chose to throw it at her.

No longer sleepy, he went to get a couple of meal bars from the fridge. He ripped one open and took a bite while watching the professor shuffle around the cab, spouting details about periods of history that left Winston in the dust.

"I mean, I get the reason why, but still. I wish you would have asked me first," Winston said to Doctor Junker around a sticky sweet mouthful.

"You were a little preoccupied at the time," the doctor reminded him, "and I couldn't risk him waking up while we were in danger."

Winston bobbed his head from side to side, unwilling to nod in agreement.

"Does he eventually calm down?" he asked, pointing his half-eaten bar at the excited older man.

"As soon as he gets the initial burst out of his system. They've suppressed his mind for so long. It's almost like watching a nanoprinter clear its job cache," Doctor Junker said while watching her brother-in-law go around the cab again.

Winston shook his head and went back to his pilot seat. A comm notification began flashing on the display, catching his attention. He flopped back into his chair.

"Let's see what we got here. Probably from Mother, since I see she took off without a goodbye," he said to himself and tapped the voicemail open.

A cultured voice came out of the speakers that made Winston think of rich vanilla cream and smooth bourbon. "Good afternoon, Baroness Junker. I have been informed you are making a layover at my little domain today and wish to invite you to afternoon tea. Please bring your brother, the captain of your vessel, and his loadmaster. It will be a lovely diversion for all while your ship is refueled. It has been so long since our last visit, and I sincerely hope you will grace my porch with your presence once again. Please RSVP so I may make the necessary arrangements."

The form opened awaiting her response.

Doctor Junker ducked back into the main cabin, having heard her name mentioned over the comm. "This is unusual," she said, a bit surprised.

"Baroness?" Winston turned around with a bit of shock on his face. "You've been underplaying your hand quite a bit, Doctor."

"Tea?" Professor Junker squealed with excitement as he rushed over to her. "We must go to tea with D. P., Amanda!"

"We shall. We shall," she said, taking his prayerfully clenched hands in hers. "Of course, we will be stopping on the way to freshen you up, Quentin. You are in a frightful state right now."

"I got a shower in the sleeper and he's welcome to a fresh flight suit if you want. Might be a bit big on him though," Winston suggested, hooking a thumb back toward the sleeper.

She looked him up and down with a frown. "You need something more fitting for tea with Commodore Roberts than that," she said, redirecting his concern.

He followed her gaze down and then pulled at the torso of his clothing. "What's wrong with my flight suit? It's expected of pilots," he griped.

She gave him a look worthy of a school marm dealing with an errant pupil. "Although that may be true most times, I would like today to be a little more dignified. We shall stop at The Grand's tailor and get some new clothes for the both of you."

"Do we have a choice?" Winston practically whined.

Doctor Junker paused for a moment as if to give deep consideration then answered, "No. First impressions are lasting impressions, and this is an important one for you."

Winston's shoulders slumped.

"Gird your loins, sir," she said with a smile. "You are going into battle like a courtier even if it is just an illusion of gaffer's tape and paste jewelry. There are politics at work here you are completely ignorant of, and that means I need you to look the part of someone in my trusted service." She looked at Billy Joe who had slid up beside Winston. "That goes for you too, Billy Joe."

"Ah," the mechoid groaned sourly.

Winston patted his shoulder in commiseration with Bubby's discontent. "Yep. That moment when you realize that there was another frying pan below to jump into after all. With a resigned grunt, he shoved the rest of the meal bar in his mouth. "Welp, let's do this right. Baroness? What's next?"

17..

On the way to the fuel dock, the *Sierra Madre's* flightpath took her over the resort side of Nova Tortuga. Unlike its original nefarious namesake, it was thousands of square miles of tropical island paradise. A large crescent-shaped lake gave the illusion of an endless ocean. Hilly skyland geography dripped with lush jungle forests, and plantations of exotic fruits and vegetables covered the plain. A large "DPR, Inc." was painted on the metal roofs of many agricultural processor buildings in large white block letters.

In the center of the crescent sat a small city that had at its heart the incredible white Gilded Age hotel, "The Grand Straits." It was surrounded by an arc of gardens that kept the rowdy pirate city at a respectful distance. The main building of the hotel was a stately behemoth with tall brilliant white colonnades creating a single front porch designed for fancy promenades.

Double-decker gazebos radiated from the porch corners, resplendent with wrought iron decorations and marble statuary. Tall, broad willows with branches weeping in fragrant blooms lined the drive leading to the hotel, while beyond them well-manicured gardens soaked in the heat of the day.

Doctor Junker smiled at the twin looks of astonishment from the pilot and loadmaster as the hotel came into view in the canopy of the *Sierra Madre*. "That is where we are having tea," she told them.

"That's a hotel? Not a palace?" Billy Joe spun around to look at her in astonishment. "I thought this place was run by pirates!"

The doctor's eyes sparkled in amusement. "In truth, it's both," she replied.

"Who would take a vacation in a place so notorious?" Winston wondered, studying the property under them as they passed by.

"You'd be surprised," she answered. "Pirates need relaxation too. Though they call it shore leave. Their coin spends just as good as a family of middle-class peasants from New Svalbard. The commodore has entertained many members of Xiao's courts. It's a delicate balance of opposing sides, but he has managed to carve out a very successful niche here. He even has a suite maintained for the Emperor if perchance the Eternal One wishes to have a pleasant visit."

"That seems kinda suicidal for a mench who's called a Pirate King," Billy Joe observed.

She shrugged lightly in response. "One man's pirate is another man's privateer," she replied. "That's something you'll have to get used to out here on the fringes. Relationships are often far more complicated than what you'd find in 'civilized' nations like the Union. One day a man's your assassin, the other he's your savior. It's why your word matters and you best keep it. Solitude can be fatal."

Winston shot her a sharp sidelong glance, then turned back to the view with a long judgmental sigh. This he did not like.

A clap of glee drew his attention. The professor pressed against the glass nose of the *Sierra Madre's* canopy, bouncing on his toes like an excited little boy. A giddy grin spread across his haggard face.

Doctor Junker noticed Winston's look of concern regarding the professor's behavior and nodded indulgently toward the older man. "Quentin and D. P. have similar loves of history, but I suspect not for the same reasons. The commodore is a bit more pragmatic than Quentin," she explained. "Still, despite the passionate discussions that can result, Quentin has always greatly enjoyed the commodore's company."

Winston glanced back at the professor then shrugged. It didn't matter, he supposed. The older man wasn't his responsibility. He turned his attention back to guiding the ship to maintain his flight path through the crowded skies.

The *Sierra Madre* flew over a gigantic fortress. At first glance it looked to be a classic waterfront pirate fort tourist trap, but as they approached Winston quickly realized those were just facades.

Underneath, it was a robust anti-airship defense network.

He hooked a thumb toward the citadel they passed. "Cute. It seems this is the commodore's way of showing off. He sure does like his guns, don't he?"

"Like any good pirate king," Doctor Junker answered. "I believe he's making sure you, as a first-time guest, understand he's well-defended and to not mess around.

"Point taken," Winston muttered.

She smoothed her skirts. "The commodore is a complex man who has many facets," she continued. "He loves good stories and treasure hunts, too. I suspect that's why he likes Quentin. To the commodore, he has been like a prized truffle-finding pig."

Winston frowned at the expression, not recognizing it, but suspected she was referring to some exotic luxury found by a grubby animal that only a rare few actually liked.

Sensing his distaste, Doctor Junker explained. "It means Quentin has sniffed out more than his fair share of profitable opportunities for the commodore without ever realizing it." A muscle tightened in her jaw as she looked at the professor. It was the first time any form of resentment had crept into her voice.

The *Sierra Madre* looped below the mist-shrouded equator's edge of Nova Tortuga, then rolled over to keep orientation as the underside was revealed. Here, the spires of heavy industry came into view, mostly made of gigantic hollow stalagmites rising from, or hanging onto, the underside of the skyland, depending on one's perspective. These towers of hardened mantle had become wharves and factory towers for processing plants. Dozens of small craft clung to the long shafts of stone that formed the natural sky harbor. Nestled in the center of the tangled formation was Winston's goal, the fueling depot.

"Not quite the den of debauchery and sin I expected," he observed as he slowed his speed for the descent into the maze.

"The commodore runs a tight ship," the professor said, "particularly close to his hotel. Once they rotate over to the dusk up top, things will get more, ahem, lively there," she said clearing her throat. "A new clientele comes out to work and play then."

Winston shook his head. "Again, I'm astonished at the rules of a pirate skyland."

The corners of her mouth rose slightly in amusement. "I'm sure most of those allegedly legitimate tugs and trains are smugglers and blackguards too. Everyone has a side hustle in the Lumina Reaches. Many irons in many fires. As long as people mind their own affairs, Nova Tortuga is like any other skyland in Xiao's empire. Minus the imperial oppression, of course," Doctor Junker explained.

Winston snorted. "Despite the open invite from the commodore to the Emperor?"

She shrugged. "He might come someday, but none of his minions would in any official capacity. Why the blindspot? I don't know. Xiao's ways are mysterious. As I explained. Relationships out here are complex," she said.

Winston wondered for the thousandth time just what he had gotten himself into as he guided his tug into the fuel dock.

The *Sierra Madre* was quietly tied up, and the fuel onload began. A decrystallizing scrub was next on her agenda. Her quartet of passengers disembarked quickly and departed for their appointment with the commodore, taking a subway through the skyland to the resort side.

The train was like a string of pearls, each car rotating to align its gravity with every station. It astounded Winston at how honeycombed the skyland was. Every quarter mile, the train stopped and people got on and off just like everywhere else. It was like being in the sprawling skyland city of Metroballus, except for the number and size of weapons people carried.

A crew of Primatoids in full battle armor carrying anti-armor cannons came aboard. No one in Winston's party put up a fuss, but they decided to change cars. Best to not be on the bullseye if something was about to go down. A few of the other passengers in their car seemed to agree and followed, the rest ignored the combat crew as nothing more than a common commuting eccentricity.

The subway reached the resort side and aligned itself accordingly then began a long circuit under the casinos and clubs of Nova Tortuga. The passengers became more colorful than dangerous, but as always, appearances were deceiving.

"I've taken the liberty to set up emergency appointments at the hotel to get us dressed for tea," Doctor Junker announced as they neared their destination.

Quentin moaned like a little boy and earned a harsh glare from his sister-in-law."When we arrive, say nothing and follow me closely. "Her tone brooked no argument. "I will take you where you need to go. Do what they say and meet me in the lobby salon after you are done. It's very important you play the part without hesitation or reservation. Are we clear?" She favored the mench in her company with a sharp look.

The three nodded.

The Grand Straits Hotel was the subway's last stop before the return trip back down. The station looked just like all the rest save for a very fancy private lift entrance, complete with doormen and awning. A concierge met them there. "Baron and Lady Junker? You are expected. Please, follow me." He led them inside the lift.

When the brass doors opened again, Winston's jaw dropped in astonishment. The Grand's lobby was a step back into old Earth's past, turn of the 19th century maybe, he guessed. The staffers were smartly dressed in either elegant black and white or militaristic red jackets and hats that bordered on the comedic. They stood silently in stoic reservation, waiting to serve, or they rushed back and forth with purpose.

Brass and crystal lighting fixtures sparkled above elegant marble checkerboard stone floors. Crimson and gold rugs lay beneath plush velvet furnishings that filled the broad hall in small, intimate arrangements. Bright white walls rose to a high ceiling with an elegant mezzanine. Soft sweet music, plucked from some historical archive, echoed through the beautiful space.

Doctor Junker put a finger to her lips with an expression that would not tolerate disobedience, then straightened up imperiously and marched them quickly through the lobby to minimize any disruption due to their incongruous appearance. She ushered them into a hallway full of various luxury services, from aestheticians and a mech-spa to haberdashers and body shops.

They were appropriately groomed and dressed in record time. Their attendants escorted them to a little salon at the services hallway entrance where Doctor Junker was already waiting for them. Winston glanced down at the unfamiliar clothing and then exchanged uneasy glances with Billy Joe. Even he was cleaned up, his exterior was buffed and polished. Winston rolled his shoulders in discomfort from his new cream and sand-colored suit and grimaced at his reflection in the glass window pane beside him. They certainly now fit their surroundings.

"I feel funny," the professor complained, tugging at his ascot, fidgeting with his own new suit.

The doctor gently but firmly pulled his hand away and held it down at his side. "I know, but remember you are the Baron now. Not your brother. There are certain expectations of nobility," she firmly reminded.

Professor Quentin groaned again. "These shoes pinch my toes."

She patted his arm reassuringly. "You're just out of practice. You've lived for years in unsightly institutional scrubs. You need to build up your tolerance for beautiful, uncomfortable clothing again," she reminded him.

"They even combed out my skirt," Billy Joe whispered to Winston, looking mortified. "I can't even hear myself moving anymore."

"Good. You've needed that for months. I'm not too crazy about this vintage getup either. I'm wearing wingtips for Xiao's sake!" Winston said, lifting his new shoe, and shaking it gingerly.

The restriction of motion in his shoulders was driving him crazy. He felt like he needed to flap his arms to get them to sit more comfortably on his frame. His new straw boater hat didn't feel right either, despite its bespoke fit.

The doctor shot him a frown. "That's not a sportsball cap, and this is not a flight onesie," she hissed and tugged on his sleeves to adjust the shoulders of Winston's jacket. She gave his hat a subtle but jaunty tilt then stood back to give him a critical look. "You're dressed like a proper gentleman for this court. And don't forget that this is a type of court. The commodore runs this slice of the Dream, and if you make a positive impression on him, you may find him a good friend to have. Just like me and the Baron," she added, nodding toward her brother-in-law.

"Yes, my lady," Winston said, sarcastically. Lifting his coattails in a sketch of a curtsey.

She ignored his mockery. "Remember to address me that way from now on," she continued primly. Giving them one last look-over, she nodded in satisfaction then swept her arm in a grand motion towards the door. "Right then. Would you gentlemench please escort me to tea? We mustn't keep the commodore waiting."

18.

A bellman led the quartet to a private gazebo at one end of the grand promenade of the hotel. As they approached, small sailboats could be seen gliding across the lake beyond. A few hundred miles above the skyland, a passing waterburg refracted the daylight, casting a rippling rainbow shadow of magical prismatic billows across the landscape.

The bellman stopped at the entrance to the arbor and stepped to the side while motioning them inside. They passed through the doorway and then paused for a moment to take in their surroundings. Gauzy curtains fluttered in the gentle afternoon breeze, filtering the bright light. Carbon Fiber Wicker furnishings topped with comfortable-looking cushions and throws filled the sheltered space. Upon a thick rug, a gilt-edged table, piled high with all manner of food and drink, took center stage. The Commodore, D. P. Roberts, one-time pirate, now turned business tycoon, stood up from his throne-like chair to greet his four guests.

"Good afternoon, Baron Junker and Lady Amanda! So good to see you again!" he smiled broadly with a bow. The smooth timber of his voice made Winston want to like him without question. A brief bolt of panic struck. Was he using a limbic manipulator on him? Could those devices cause sensations of trust? Did Holly manipulate him this way too? He lost sense of where he was as he fought to get his breathing under control.

Doctor Junker reached her hand out toward their host. "Commodore, it has been a while since we last visited. Thank you for the invitation," she said as he kissed her pastel yellow satin glove.

Roberts went to the professor next and gave a small bow of respect, then stuck out a firm hand. "My dear, Quentin! Oh, wait. Begging your pardon. Baron Junker, I should say! Glad to have you back among the living!"

The professor started a little at the greeting and then remembered his new status and took the offered hand with enthusiasm. "I suppose I am back among the living! Yes, yes! Glad to be back. I look forward to having more talks again soon, but first I have so much research left to others in my absence to check on," he gushed, shaking the commodore's hand with both of his and with even greater enthusiasm.

"I look forward to it," the commodore said, his delight sounding genuine. He then turned to Winston. "And you must be the pilot who aided Lady Amanda and the Baron. Nahqing proud of you, son. It takes a brave man to stick his neck out for someone like old Professor Q as you did."

The praise surprised Winston, snapping him back to the present. He shrugged lightly. "Uh... thank you, Commodore," he said meekly. "It was nothing, really. Something any good person would do."

"Ha!" the commodore clapped his shoulder heartily. "Then there is an absolute dearth of good people in the Dream. Perhaps old Emperor Xiao has them all in prison? Leaving only scalawags like me to run amok out there!" He blasted out a self-deprecating laugh.

Winston smiled at the bombastic man's wink. He noted that there was none of the familiar itching in his brain caused by a limbic manipulator. Perhaps this man was just that naturally charismatic? He supposed he must be to earn the title of Commodore. Not to mention have the power to keep it despite his peers who would kill for his place. Winston gave a quiet relieved sigh, unnoticed by their host who had turned to the final member of their party

"I'm sorry to say, I didn't get your name, son. If you're part of this captain's crew, you are most welcome at my table," the commodore said, giving his hand over to the big indu.

"I go by Billy Joe, sir," the mechoid answered while shaking the offered hand. "I'm Winston's loadmaster, mechanic, general handyman and muscle." He added the last part with a wink.

The commodore burst out with a loud guffaw. "Behind every great pilot is someone who makes it all happen. Am I right?" He gave Billy Joe a chuck on his soft nanosand shoulder.

"Winston and I are a team, sir, so I'd say we got each other's back," Billy Joe said, a little puffed with pride.

Commodore Roberts gave him a surprised smile and looked back at Winston. "You got one heck of an indu for a partner, Captain Winston. Purg of a mench. I'd hang on to him for dear life," and he slapped Billy Joe on the back. Leaning in close, he whispered loud enough for everyone to hear, "Let me know if you're looking for a bigger opportunity, my good mench."

"Thank y'all, but no, Commodore. Me and Winston are sticking it out." Winston bet if Billy Joe had been capable of blushing, he would have been bright red. As it was, his face still managed to convey his embarrassed pleasure.

The commodore shrugged with a large sigh. "My loss, I guess. Assuming I can't get the pair of you to work for me someday," he shot them a saucy wink as he walked to his table. "Now, please, have a seat. Let us enjoy the rest of the afternoon together and talk about how you gained your freedom. I must have your first-hand accounts."

The afternoon drifted into twilight and the skyland's dusk side took hold. From a distance, the sounds of a wild and boisterous night drifted in on the light breeze. The bordellos, casinos and a veritable carnival of other violent amusements re-animated in the growing shade, like vampires waking up to feed.

Winston and Billy Joe told the commodore a highly edited tale of their escape from the Black Void to the rescue of the Bonavitae clinic lill they arrived, keeping the action high and specifics low. The commodore never once challenged or pressed for detail. He listened carefully and occasionally punctuated the tale with enthusiastic encouragement.

"I wonder who was the pirate captain you skunked?" the commodore mused.

"No idea, but I hope to never meet them again, or if I do, I pray that neither of us knows it," Winston answered.

A red pillbox-capped bellman came to the gazebo steps. He carried a silver tray bearing four sealed envelopes.

"Excuse me, Commodore. A set of messages for you and your party." The man bowed in apology for his disruption. He was given a nod of permission, and with expert economy, he presented the envelopes to each in their order. One to D. P. Roberts, another addressed to Doctor Junker, the third to Billy Joe and the last to Winston. All were paper pockets, nanofabricated in a closed state so no one could tamper with the contents. There was not even a seal to break. They had to be torn open to read. Each name was printed in fancy calligraphy.

"My, my! Entertaining tales and a mystery!" the commodore said. He gave his envelope a shake next to his ear, hearing something light slide around in the sealed envelope. "How did we come by these?" he asked the bellman.

"They were delivered to the front desk by four different couriers. It seems they arrived from all over Nova Tortuga. One came off the last bulk-freight dirigibles just before she departed," the bellman replied.

"So curious. Scanned?" The commodore asked his employee, giving the envelope a sniff.

"Absolutely, Commodore. No threats found."

"Then that will be all," the commodore dismissed the man with a wave. The bellman clicked his heels and walked briskly down the brightly lit promenade, tipping his hat to a couple taking in the evening air, and disappeared back inside.

Once alone, the commodore looked to Lady Amanda and pointed his nose towards the package in her hand. "Would you care to open yours first, my Lady?"

She tapped it a few times to settle the smaller message onto one end then tore open the opposite side. She gave it a little shake to dislodge the delicate note and a card-sized piece of translucent paper fell into her palm. It was covered with dots and small lines with a crosshair mark on a corner. The professor leaned over from his place beside her and looked curiously at the patterns printed on it.

"Is it a code?" the commodore asked, tearing his open to find the same size sheet with similar dots and hash marks on his.

"I've no idea," the professor mused. "It's not any system of language, code, or pictogram I've seen before."

Winston pulled out his card made of the same translucent paper. All the patterns were unique, but in the lower corner of his message was a large black square about the size of his thumb and the words "Touch me" beneath it.

"Mine says the same, Hoss," Billy Joe said, holding his up.

Billy Joe touched the square, and some of the markings began to glow, but nothing else.

Winston did the same but nothing happened. "Could mine be broken?" he wondered aloud.

"I do not understand," the commodore stroked the corners of his mustache in contemplation.

Everyone puzzled over the strange papers. Only Billy Joe managed to cause the square on his piece to glow.

"Ah hah!" Lady Amanda suddenly clapped her hands. "It's not a code, it's a circuit for something else! Give me your papers," she commanded, collecting the squares and piling them on top of one another. "It's a printable circuit. One square is a power input, the other must be authentication."

For a few minutes, she worked to align the pieces of paper. She tried a variety of patterns until the cards fanned out at precise angles and the alignment crosshairs matched. The effect revealed what looked like a chip design and memory circuits.

"Incredible!" the professor whispered in awe.

"Billy Joe," Doctor Junker said softly as if speaking too loud would cause the design to fall apart. "Hold these in this alignment, then touch your square." Billy Joe did as he was asked, and the whole pattern began to glow a dim red. Doctor Junker clutched her brother's hand with a triumphant squeal.

"Now, Winston, authorize the message," she begged.

Winston placed his thumb on the other square.

Nothing.

They all let out a defeated sigh.

Like a ghostly Will o' the Wisp, words materialized in the air above the paper.

"Your most important finger."

They stared at the phrase, astonished.

"A nanoscopic holoprojector? Incredible!" Lady Amanda gasped.

"This reference is beyond me," Commodore Roberts leaned back in his chair and lit a cigar. "But this is nahq exciting."

"What's the most important finger, Hoss?" Billy Joe asked, keeping contact with the square.

"I would guess my index finger on my right hand?" Winston pressed again with that finger.

The words changed.

"**YOUR** most important finger. One try left."

"What the purg?" Winston cried out in frustration. "Eight choices but only one's right, and if I blow it, what? Some sort of self-destruct?"

"Calm down, Winston," Doctor Junker instructed. "This is specific to you. Someone sent this who knows that one finger on one of your hands is more important than your thumb or trigger finger. What could that possibly mean to you?"

Winston froze, his face draining of color. Only two people knew what this could have meant. One was sitting beside him, powering this self-immolating holoprojector, and the other was Mother.

He gulped down the last of his highball, and slowly stretched out his left hand. With a deep breath, he pressed the tip of his ring finger to the authenticator. The circuit pattern went from red to cool green, the glow intensifying as it drew more power with activation.

A miniature image of Mother appeared between Winston and Billy Joe's hands.

"Commodore Roberts, Baroness Junker, Winston, Billy Joe," the little avatar message greeted her assumed audience. Mother's voice caused the paper to quake like a speaker, making it tinny and distorted. "I am sorry to have left you in such a situation, but I had to reintegrate with my prime self without delay. If I calculated our situation correctly there will not be much time for me to act. Considering the events of our recent escapade, you are most likely receiving this message due to my untimely destruction."

"No," Winston gasped.

Lady Amanda's hand flew to her mouth in horror.

The commodore blew out a cloud of smoke, giving the hologram a touch of fairy fire.

"No doubt I have run so far afoul with Xiao that he will take action against me for my gambit, of which you were a small part, has failed. Since it is my fault to have put you in such precarious straits, I have chosen to do everything I could to protect you and make amends. Hopefully, this will preserve what is yours, so you can start over."

"I assume you are viewing this with Commodore Roberts. To him, I would ask for his favor to be given to you in case you restart your professional life here. If he agrees, a token of my thanks will be provided to him through the Baroness."

"He shall have it if he asks," the commodore said to the recording.

"To the Baroness Junker, I ask her to remain your patroness and give you both a new home in the Lumina Reaches."

Lady Amanda nodded, agreeing to the wish.

"I shall also be sending you a gift in connection to this request," Mother continued. "Winston, Billy Joe, it will be of great benefit to you. There is a strong probability you can use it with the professor for whom much was unknowingly sacrificed. May you all do something great with it.

"I am transferring all funds you have on my corporate books to your Curre-Gram account. Here is the express code.

A long alpha-numeric string and symbols burned into the top copy of the paper.

"This will allow you to cash out your account in hard currency from any Curre-Gram affiliated office. Do not transfer the money electronically. Take physical delivery only."

"Once you have the physical currency, purchase as much precious metal, gems, or rare earths as you can get for it as soon as you can, no matter the market price. Preferably do this before you leave the same place you pick up your cash. Money can be tracked. Even physical cash. I know you're not used to thinking this way, but trust me. This will break the financial chain of custody and you will be safe from any financial tracking." Mother nervously rubbed her hands together, her sad frown desperate.

"She's not wrong there," the commodore confirmed. "I believe we can aid you on this too."

"Do not try to contact me. If I survived, I will get in touch with you as soon as I can. You do not want what is coming for me to start hunting you. You will have to sacrifice the *Sierra Madre*. Xiao and Bonavitae are certainly both searching for it. With the funds above, you will have the money for a new vessel to continue your trade. Name her well."

The worried little icon of Mother clasped her hands together, almost pleading.

"Follow this plan, Winston. Stay hidden with Doctor Junker, and hope that my suspicions of what is about to happen to me are wrong. It's not often I feel a connection with a human like yourself and it has been a pleasure working with you. I hope we get the chance to do so again in the future."

With that, she vanished in a dusting of flickering green pixels followed briefly by a signature: MotherRoad.

"I don't believe it!" The commodore slapped his free hand against the table. "I never knew the Motherroad Corporation was sentient! That dataoid's been around since the arrival of the Dream! It's massive!" He laughed and slapped the table again. "I've pillaged so many of her transports and warehouses over the years I've lost count, and now she drops her favorites into my very lap, with my good friends? And gives me gifts? Doesn't this beat all? Now, this is a story for the ages!"

He leaned back and laughed at the ceiling.

Winston didn't feel quite the same ironic gaiety that the pirate king did. It was clear that neither Billy Joe nor Lady Amanda did as well.

Noticing the silence, Roberts looked at his guests. "Why the glum faces?"

"Mother… or MotherRoad is gone. Xiao killed her," Billy Joe said.

"Balderdash," the commodore declared, waving a hand in dismissal. He sat puffing his cigar in contemplation of the news, then leaned toward them intently.

The glowing tip of his cigar gave his face a devilish cast in the dim light of the Nova Tortuga dusk. "To quote an old pirate homily, we pirates are never more dangerous than when we're dead. And let me tell you something else that's true. Baron and Lady, Captain and Loadmaster… MotherRoad was a pirate all the way to her core. You shall see."

#   #   #

INTERLUDE: XIAO SNAPS THE REIGNS

1.

"Enough!" Marshal Dynne barked to his bridge crew. "Move in and let's do our duty. Let these traitors know we're coming, pilot."

"Hail Xiao," came the enthusiastic response from the bridge crew. The pilot fired up the grav fans to full blast. It took less than a minute for the warjet to make the jaunt from its listening post to the 18th hole of the Baqqan Club golf course.

Marshal Dynne's pilot timed it perfectly. The thunderclap did not destroy property but would scare the purg out of those nearby. They were enforcing imperial law, not performing a military operation. Wanton destruction was not warranted.

The hot sky above the elite resort of the Baqqan Club rattled with the imperial warjet's arrival. Startled eyes looked up to see the dark arrowhead of Xiao's navy coasting to a stop over the 18th green. Nervous faces peeked from the clubhouse windows. Staffers ran for shelter in the basement security bunker leaving panicked guests to fend for themselves.

Below, the Marquis of Yevgenni, the High Judge of Gaxsony, his corporate guests and a substantial security entourage could only stare, exposed and helpless at the brutal symbol of Xiao's power. Hands flashed for holsters and into jackets to draw their sidearms. Instantly, anti-personnel turrets on the warjet pointed at those who dared reach for their weapons.

"Stand down, mench!" the High Judge, Marquis of Yevgenni ordered. They reluctantly obeyed.

Marshal Dynne smirked as he watched the marquis try to look the peaceful innocent.

The airship slid sideways around the party in a low looping circle, guns tracking true, and set down between the clubhouse and the green. Crackling fans bathed everyone in their hot ionized exhaust before shutting down.

"Security detail, on me," Marshal Dynne snapped, getting up from his command chair and donning his helmet. "Let's make some arrests."

The bow cargo ramp dropped open like a gaping maw. A quartet of waroids jogged out, muskets and l-ray scribblers up, their deep blue corundumite armor glinting in the sun. Marshal Dynne descended the ramp with long, gallant strides. More troopers followed in his wake.

The High Judge of Gaxsony lifted his jaw a hair and using his putter as a cane, rested his right hand on the tip of the grip as the marshal approached. Marshal Dynne's hands flashed up into the imperial salute, his stern gaze peeking through his splayed fingers that mimicked the Eye of the Eternal One.

"Hail Xiao! Source of all truth and justice!" Marshal Dynne challenged all in the entourage.

Slowly, all hands of those on the golf outing went up to return the salute. "Hail Xiao!" they repeated.

Marshal Dynne's smile hardened at their tepid obedience and lack of fervor.

"Lord High Judge, Marquis of Yevgenni, I have come to place you and your party under arrest. Comply and may Xiao's justice fall gently upon you," Marshal Dynne said. He always loved adding that last phrase. It gave the prisoners false hope. The imperial torturers may not like it, because their subjects fought harder, but that was not his concern.

"On what grounds?" complained one of the corporate guests. His superior, Monsieur Fahn Dangalde, Executive Vice President of Bonavitae Pharmaceuticals spun in his flight harness. He gave the complainer a withering look.

"You worthless jackal!" he rebuked. His secretary turned on the one who spoke and, gave him a chop to the back of the neck, then swept his knees bringing the man to the ground. Marshal Dynne blinked in surprise as the secretary knelt on the neck of the other. She looked up, awaiting her boss's orders.

Monsieur Dangalde floated between the sudden attack he ordered and the marshal's hard gaze. "Forgive us, Marshal. This one forgot his place. Hail Xiao." The bloated man gave a strange floating bow. "Shall I have him dispatched for such insolence toward the Eternal One?"

Dangalde's eyes focused past the marshal to see the waroid rifles locked on them.

With a squint of the eyes, Marshal Dynne turned to the High Judge of Saxony. "I do not have time to deal with this foolishness. Your fates will be sorted out in Xiao's courts. Take them to the holding cells," he ordered his troops.

There was loud complaining as every member of the entourage was seized. The waroids forced them at gunpoint up the ramp into the airship. Marshal Dynne with his bodyguards and the High Judge stayed on the green, unwavering, like two arrogant gunslingers, certain in their righteous cause.

"You know who I am," the Marquis of Yevgenni stated flatly.

"I do," Marshal Dynne said. The fool, he thought. He believes there is some way out for him. Does he smell the scent of corruption on me? How pathetic.

"Then you know by Xiao's law, as a Courtier of the Eighth Array, you cannot lay hands on me. Not without known sufficient cause," the high judge said. His voice was firm, but not strident, in the knowledge of his rights and privileges.

The pin flag snapped and fluttered in the hand of the petrified golf caddy. From the clubhouse, a gallery of members and servants had come out of hiding to the luncheon patio to witness the arrest.

"You wish a public listing of your charges against the Emperor?" Marshal Dynne said boldly, casting an eye over his shoulder at the throng of witnesses. The whispering crowd eagerly awaited to hear the scandalous reasons for the arrest of a high judge.

"I will be found innocent of every charge," the marquis proclaimed.

Marshal Dynne's chilly smile seemed to not affect the jurist.

"As you wish," he agreed. He loved it when they demanded a public reading of their crimes. "You are hereby charged with conspiracy and rebellion against the Empire. Furthermore, you are charged with lending aid and comfort to rebel forces and criminals, accepting and paying bribery and colluding with other enterprises to defraud the legal system and cover up crimes committed in secret against the Eternal One. These crimes are equivalent to high treason against Xiao the Eternal, and carry the punishment of death by public execution in a manner he deems the most... appropriate... to the Empire's needs."

The Marquis of Yevgenni was too well-bred and practiced to show more than a flicker of worry on his face. That flicker gave a little thrill to Marshal Dynne's spirit.

"If," the marshal warned, "you resist arrest it will be considered proof of your guilt, and I will have the privilege of executing you here and now." He slipped his sidearm out from his holster.

A bead of sweat rolled down the high judge's nose and dangled from its tip, clinging to it while growing more ponderous only to be wiped away by the high judge the instant before it fell. It took all of Marshal Dynne's resolve to not smile.

"I am at your disposal, Marshal," the high judge agreed, his eyes dropping from the lawman.

"Hail Xiao," came Marshal Dynne's smug mutter. With a jerk of his head, a pair of his bodyguards cuffed the High Judge of Gaxsony and escorted him up the ramp to the holding cells.

Marshal Dynne took in a deep breath and let it out slowly. His smile grew as it ended. With a crisp turn to the petrified Baqqan Club caddy, he gave a very slight bow. "Enjoy your day, denizen."

The caddy flinched but did not flee. "Ha-hail Xiao," came the stuttering reply.

Marshal Dynne strode up the ramp of his warjet in long confident strides, and they lifted off, vanishing from sight with the sound of thunder.

2.

In the harem garden, floating meditation bowls rang softly on pristine blue pools. Ripples of light danced among colorful silk banners hundreds of feet long. They vanished into the tower above, gently swirling in the jasmine-scented air. Thrust up from among the secluded nooks stood diamond-shaped, artistically-broken pillars like giant styli that mirrored the rays of the imperial crest.

In private hidden sanctuaries were beds and couches perfect for intimate tête-à-têts. The harem was replete with exotic women of the most astounding beauty. Unique in every flavor of femininity save for one unifying feature: a startling imperial blue left eye that shone like lightning and sapphires. The feature was bestowed upon them as a gift and brand from their lover, the Emperor, Xiao the Eternal.

A woman of regal bearing lay under the covers of a bed of satin and fur. Compared to the exotic beauties that inhabited the harem, she was almost plain, like a jade statuette in a pile of perfect gems, beautiful but incongruous.

Her skin was radiant with the afterglow of lovemaking, but her lips were pinched tight. The rendezvous tainted her mind with a residue of shame. She consoled herself with her noble sacrifice, but that only deepened her self-loathing. Despite her lover's rumored reputation, he had been kind, thoughtful and responsive to her needs. He knew precisely how to drive her to ecstasy. It was an experience she knew she would cherish and hate for the rest of her life, which made her despise him all the more.

Emperor Xiao had demanded her for one day and one night as tribute from her husband's duchy, proof that anything he possessed could be taken by Emperor Xiao's whim. The consequences to his people would have been catastrophic if she refused. Her husband had been ready to pay the price for his pride and her honor, but she would not hear of it. Her body became a shield for the innocent. With this act of obedience, the Emperor would not blast her husband's duchy and their people would not be enslaved.

Her lover, Xiao the Eternal knelt above her on one knee. He curled up the ends of his mustache and stroked his thin soul patch. His fingers drifted down to stroke her cheek tenderly.

"My eye," the noblewoman moaned as she stirred in her musings. "It itches."

"Of course it does," Xiao said. "All women who know my touch receive the gift."

She looked up at him. Tears welled up but she remained silent.

"It is not so bad, my pet," Xiao said tenderly. "In nine months, you will serve the second part of your tribute to me."

The noblewoman was paralyzed by his words, eyes glittering as if her tears had frozen.

"My flower already grows for my seed has taken hold." His finger traced around her eye in a strange pattern. "I shall gather my harvest in thirteen years when you present my child to me.

Then, I will take him into my household, and you can return to the way you were."

Xiao stood up and, adjusting his sword and pistol, gave a self-satisfied sigh.

"Now I must attend to affairs of the court, as must you," the Emperor said, walking away. As soon as Xiao was gone, she scrambled on her hands and knees off the sumptuous mattress to the water's edge and gazed into her reflection. The electric sapphire blue of her left eye stared back.

As she watched, a tattoo grew around her eye. A line drawing of an exotic flower encircled the socket and made her look even more exotic. The design grew painlessly, turning into a long winding stem with ornate flower buds and leaves that coiled around her neck like a collar, then coursed down between the valley of her breasts and to her navel, marking where Xiao had planted his seed.

Though the tattoo would fade over the years, every time her husband would look at her face, he would see Xiao's eye staring back, taunting him with what the Eternal Emperor could demand

and must be willingly given if there ever was a next time.

Her anguished scream disappeared into the folds of the endless banners above. The Eternal Emperor had lingered at the door just long enough to listen and smiled. With a chuckle, he joined his imperial guard and walked jauntily toward his court.

3.

"Prisoners!" the loud synthetic voice barked. "Embark the barge!"

Marshal Dynne heard the guard's command echo down the dungeon corridor to him. A smile crept across his lips as he finished the last page of prisoner transfer paperwork. He handed it back to the desk sergeant at the control point. Whistling a soft cadence to himself, he walked toward the source of the commanding voice with a jaunty step.

The prisoner barge was docked to a catwalk that jutted out into a large empty shaft that had no bottom. A mechoid pilot waited at his control podium on the barge. Six elite waroids perched on the corners of the hexagonal floating platform. Their octopus-like nanosand tentacles coiled around the corner plinths. Their heads were a pair of Janus-like masks. Beautiful, idyllic and emotionless, they stared in opposite directions, each controlling their own set of nanosand arms that held large energy rifles at the ready.

Marshal Dynne turned to see the Baqqan Club arrestees trudging toward him out of the cell block tunnel bracketed by a quartet of guards. They gave him bitter looks as they passed by and climbed aboard. He drew a deep breath with immense satisfaction.

The Marquis de Yevgenni was the first on board. Monsieur Fahn Dangalde, former Vice President of Operations for Bonavitae Pharmaceuticals, followed. His face ran with agonized sweat due to his atrophied back and weak legs that were almost unable to carry the ponderous bulk of his flesh.

Marshal Dynne supposed walking only a few yards from his holding cell to the barge was torture for a being who lived for years in a flight rig. The barge sagged a fraction of an inch from the extreme mass of Monsieur Dangalde as he took his place on the raised center of the barge's floating platform.

Securing rods extended up from the floor and sprouted utility liquid tentacles that wrenched the prisoners' wrists back, tethering them to the barge. The rotund vice president groaned as he discovered the rods offered little aid in standing and falling would dislocate both his shoulders.

"Is everything set?" Marshal Dynne asked the barge pilot standing in front at the controls.

"All is ready, Marshal. Your audience will begin in a few moments," the auto-tuned pilot's voice said. The eerie two-faced guard nodded.

"Praise Xiao," Dynne said with soft relish and stepped on the barge and took his position. There was a soft bump as the prisoner barge released its docking clamps and floated to its staging point. He could see nothing but the dim light coming from the corridor illuminating them like a faint spotlight as they waited in the void.

From somewhere in the dark of the shaft came faint reverberating applause to an indistinct announcement. Then followed a much more clear trio of "Hail Xiao! Hail!" cheers.

Marshal Dynne suspected the Magistrate of the Eighth Array was listing the charges against his prisoners. Dynne stretched his jaw and massaged his cheeks. They were tight from all his smiling. The compliments and well wishes from his superiors in Imperial Security since his arrival grew his pride.

A slow angry swell of voices came from the court somewhere above him. Then the first low notes vibrated the barge as the Dirge for the Accused filled the air. Light bloomed above as an opening like a flower bloomed. It was shown like light through a stained glass window upon the barge as the blackness above parted. A great circle of frosted glass floor was revealed. Shapes of people standing on it made the light ripple and dancc.

As the dirge crescendoed, the barge began to rise. Mist poured through the floor as an opening grew, timed to the swelling music. They floated up into the midst of the Court of the Eighth Array with a fountain of fog bursting around them. A plethora of optical effects lit the vapor. The barge hovered just over the heads of the parted crowd of peerage, courtiers and guests who gasped and grumbled at their entrance.

The chambers were a kaleidoscope of hundreds of representatives with myriad titles and ceremonial dress. They came with their attendants and entourages to witness the spectacle.

Dynne luxuriated in the gazes, striking the pose he knew on an innate level was expected of him. The noble lawman, a righteous hand of Xiao's justice. He lifted his chin and let an aloof and dangerous cast settle on his features.

Courtiers on all sides milled and buzzed in a subtle fervor to glance and whisper their opinions with one another. The private data feeds glowed white hot with all their gossip and theories of what was to come. The marshal saw all the hungry eyes flavored with smirks as they looked upon his prisoners. Knowing nods grew as the throng leered at the prisoner who was once their own. Their hearts already judged him, calculating a way to profit from his misfortune. When the barge moved forward out of the spectacle of light and mist, Marshal Dynne was able to take in all his surroundings.

The court was surrounded by walls of the thickest glass. Patterns caused by light refraction became visible as the barge moved. Beyond the reinforcing arches of ornamented diamond and metal glass, a bizarre ecosystem existed. Xiao's private nature reserve whose species were a cross between fungus, animal and plant that defied explanation. Creatures made of crystalline silica bone and silicone flesh flourished here. Translucent, luminous bodies intertwined and spread, coexisting in manners Marshal Dynne hoped never to see again.

Then, there he was before him! Emperor Xiao! The All-Seeing Eye! Marshal Dynne's mouth went dry. His heart seemed to lose rhythm at the sight of his sovereign. His back stiffened as he tried to look even more perfect for his liege. He blinked his eyes, pained with fighting back the emotion at the sight of the demigod upon whom all mankind's survival rested. There was the sudden urge to laugh uncontrollably and he hoped no one would ask him to speak.

The emperor reclined upon his throne with a lazy air of indifference to the approach of the barge and its prisoners while all other eyes locked onto the accused. The Chamberlain of the Eighth Array bowed low, bringing his ear close to listen to his master's words over the thundering music and angry rumble of the court.

Xiao finished speaking to his chamberlain and a collection of beautiful women from his many harems attended to him. The winetaster did her duty and poured a new drink. Exotic finger food was served to him as he blithely took in the spectacle of the prisoner barge skimming slowly over the heads of his courtiers, approaching the imperial stage. He watched his emperor take another bite that looked to be more interesting to him than the importance of judgment on the captured prisoners.

A bitter thought suddenly pestered Marshal Dynne at the sight. He squashed it down before it could do more than glimmer in his mind.

Before the throne, the Sergeant at Arms stood at attention between the emperor and his court with a company of Glassmen. The glistening human figures of cobalt glass, looking like arpeggiated notes on a musical staff, stood on the five steps of the dais. A dim ethereal light shone deep in their core. Pale points of light created the hint of two chartreuse eyes, constantly tracking about the room, tightening to sharp candle-like pinpricks if anything seemed to warrant deeper scrutiny.

The barge came to a stop a few yards from the throne as the last beat of the Dirge for the Accused ended.

"Hail Xiao!" came the command from the court magistrate as his hands flashed up into the imperial salute. The hands of all the courtiers flashed up in front of their faces, right over left, palm to palm, fingers fanned out with their thumbs pointing up and down.

"Hail Xiao! Hail!" thundered the reply.

The court magistrate stepped officiously before the throne. "Prisoners!" he addressed the barge as spotlights snapped onto the floating hexagon. His amplified voice slapped sharply off the panes of glass. "The evidence against you has been scrutinized by the Imperial Court. Your own actions are weighed and found wanting on the scales of justice. Witnesses to your crimes have come forward and testified against you and their words have been deemed true and accurate by Xiao's interrogation."

Videos of security intakes of the witnesses shone behind the throne for the benefit of the court. There were dozens. Marshal Dynne's awe at the spectacle twisted into a vindictive needle of pride. The doctors, nurses and orderlies he rescued confessed their crimes and complicity with the enemies of Xiao.

If only he had caught that opportunistic smuggler who had dropped them all at his feet during the Blaugarten Black Void event. To have caught him as well would have been the brightest jewel for his personal honor. To have chased the stolen weapons cache for weeks only to have it all declared destroyed and the last criminal escaped was like a scar on his face that could not be repaired.

If not for the fight with Bonnie Prince Charlie, he'd have caught him, too. Gathering up the free-floating containers could have waited and catching the Bonavitae frigate was childsplay. So the smallest fish named Winston Harper slipped his net. Perhaps their paths would cross again. Till then, he would have to be satisfied with executing the terrorist, Mr. Tollman.

Marshal Dynne's eyes were drawn by the movement of his lounging emperor who sprawled, disinterested and took another delicacy from a nearly naked woman. A sliver of icy offense slid into Marshal Dynne's mind as the emperor ignored his achievement.

The court magistrate went on, "Because of the willing cooperation of these witnesses who provided evidence to imperial justice, their lives will be graciously spared. Xiao, in his eternal grace, has commuted their sentence to life in servitude where they will be used as needed as reparation for the harm they caused the Empire."

Marshal Dynne was surprised at the judgment. He was expecting a much more nuanced sentence for those who worked for Bonavitae but were caught in the crossfire. At least their skills will have use elsewhere in the empire, he thought to himself. Medical personnel won't be sent to the Mines of Ditafrizt.

The real traitors were now in custody before Xiao. Most had been innocent of the activities of their superiors, serving the legitimate needs of their corporate masters. Perhaps something more was discovered by the imperial torturers his investigation had not turned up? That might have been the reason he was told to stand down when he asked permission to pursue the mystery woman who had inserted herself into this drama so early on.

The court magistrate continued, "Monsieur Fahn Dangalde. You are charged with high treason. Investigations into your activities have revealed a network of illegal medical facilities providing aid and comfort to numerous terrorist cells and rebels contending with the Empire. Your bio-weapons program at your facility in the Gaxsony Skylands was discovered during an investigation of events surrounding the Blaugarten Black Void event. Evidence obtained by physical and data searches proved you were creating toxic genesplice super soldiers for the Prince of Rrre'Dibit. The Prince is in disfavor, due to his support for the rebellion against the Empire. This constitutes a capital offense."

On the holoprojections, documents and charts that Marshal Dynne had discovered among the smuggler's captured containers were displayed. Video excerpts of the mangled and floating amphiboid abominations he secured were shown briefly. A video of one of his deputies nearly dying after coming in contact with one of the amphiboid corpses displayed in the air. The court collectively choked in disgust at the images of the biochemically maimed deputy.

Marshal Dynne watched the emperor closely. HIs eyes were methodically locking on specific members of his court, scrutinizing their reactions with terrible focus. Dynne felt a cold pang of disappointment deep in his belly. Did not the emperor care about his exemplary work? He had destroyed a significant rebel operation!

More images of incriminating evidence obtained by Imperial Data Security appeared on holograms. The Motherroad logo showed on many documents.

Then came transcripts of Doctor O'Chaudry, the facility director's torture session. Marshal Dynne smiled at the memories of his cries and anguish. A faint unpleasant smell wafted from Monsieur Dangalde who finally made the connections to how thoroughly he was betrayed by a bevy of his co-conspirators, and he snarled a low growl of impotent fury at the Marquis de Yovgenni. He was their scapegoat.

"Your Majesty," the court magistrate finally concluded after a lengthy list of other charges and turned to the emperor, "Would you like to partake of your imperial privilege of official comment?"

Xiao perked up and rose elegantly from his throne. With a spring to his step, he descended the dais to be just above eye level with Monsieur Dangalde. The man stiffened as the emperor stopped before him. Those impossible imperial blue eyes seemed to cut through the man's flesh and into his soul.

"From the bearing of the hippo's posture, I see he is not repentant of his crimes. Even if pushed to recant by my most skilled torturer, he would still resume his treasonous ways," Xiao said. The tone in which he spoke caused a bitter chill to shoot down Marshal Dynne's spine.

"He has provided aid and comfort to animals who are my enemies. Therefore, it is good he dies like an animal... for our entertainment. It will be instructional for all those who exist in my grace to observe the consequence of being a traitor.

Therefore, broadcast his demise every day for a week across all feeds as a reminder to those who might consider taking up arms against the empire."

Monsieur Dangalde let forth a screech of indignation. The words vanished in the court's roar of approval as he proved the emperor's evaluation of his unrepentant heart.

"Expel this refuse," Xiao commanded with a flip of his hand.

Dynne's eyes went wide as the barge slid forward a few feet and tilted rapidly backward. He grabbed the waist hook on his post to keep himself from falling as well. Monsieur Dangalde's post released its restraints and retracted back into the barge deck. The quarter-ton fat man fell back with a wet slap and tumbled off the barge. A split second before his bulk was about to smack into the milky glass floor like a turkey carcass, it rippled open into a chute and swallowed him up like a hungry mouth, then vanished.

The court cheered as the barge righted itself again. Xiao returned to his throne and the excitement died low, anticipating what was to come. All eyes refocused on the Marquis de Yevgenni, waiting breathlessly for the sentence to come.

The court magistrate strode forward, feeling the support of the court. His mouth opened but the Marquis de Yevgenni, High Judge of Gaxsony shouted first, cutting off the magistrate.

"By Xiao's Seventeenth Law of Peerage, I demand my right to imperial mediation!"

The high judge's voice was sharp and clear, echoing back off the far-off walls of the room.

Xiao paused in mid-bite of an exotic dessert before finishing his mouthful with a crispy crunch. He turned to face his marquis with an arched eyebrow and a pique of interest. The microphones picked up the emperor's lip-smacking as he finished his treat, dabbed the crumbs from his lips and stood up again. Marshal Dynne was sure it was not anger on his Majesty's face, but sour amusement.

"And you think such a privilege as protection under my Laws of Peerage still includes you?" The emperor's words were light on the ear. Teasing, fragile.

"Sentence has not been passed, ergo, I still retain my rights in this august court, Your Majesty," the high judge replied confidently.

Marshal Dynne could scarcely breathe. The audacity of this prisoner! The Court of the Eighth Array murmured in agitated alignment with the Marshal.

Emperor Xiao stood up and stepped down the dais again toward the barge. His lips gained the faintest hint of a smile.

"Well, it seems I shall have more than a bit of idle amusement and tedium today!" he said and came down to a step even with the barge, gesturing for it to pull forward. A pair of imperial guard Glassman stepped forward to follow, hands crooked into dangerous-looking claws of glowing glass tines, eyes trending toward a sunny orange, swirls of light coursing through their bodies.

The barge obeyed and came forward. Marshal Dynne moved out of the way of his master with a low bow and salute and faint "Hail Xiao."

The emperor stepped on board with the pair of Glassmen. He looked at the pilot and they quickly rose halfway up and flew toward the wall. A portal opened up like a rose window in a cathedral. They passed out into the nature preserve beyond.

4..

The air smelled like a blend of epoxy, flatulence and hot beach sand. Marshal Dynne's eyes watered with the first wave of the stench and he could not help but raise the back of his hand to his nose in an effort to ward off the pain. Emperor Xiao seemed unphased by the pungent, humid atmosphere.

"The smell of a Silicane environment takes some time getting used to," he said to Marshal Dynne. The lawman's eyes snapped wide open as his god-emperor casually spoke to him about such a trivial matter.

"It seems so, Your Majesty," he answered weakly to his smiling monarch.

The bound Marquis de Yevgenni whipped his head back and forth in a futile attempt to escape the scent.

"You should be thankful," Xiao told the Marquis. "I don't let many sentients come with me on a tour. Pilot, Take us for a little spin and show off my sanctuary to my guests," Xiao said.

The pilot mutely agreed and raised the barge up over the mushroom trees of latticed silica. Large gasbag-like creatures floated leisurely in the light breeze. Their huge distended bladders were like hot air balloons with fleshy carriages of bodies hanging down, dripping with long limbs that scrabbled and clawed at anything they touched, pulling it to their mouths.

One came too close to the barge. Three of the Janus-faced guards opened fire with their guns while the other side remained pointed toward the prisoner. P-beams, fried the sky between them and the aggressive creature. Thunder cracks from artificial lightning were followed by a low rumbling whoosh from the ruptured sack. Nearly invisible blue flames of burning hydrogen flared through the wounds, and the creature fell in a fireball to the ground below. Its hard body parts smashed like china plates in a bag of gelatin.

"A little more caution, pilot," was all Xiao admonished, and put a foot up on the hexagonal railing.

The barge floated a little higher and kept a more respectable distance from those monsters. The air up here was better to Marshal Dynne's taste. It was cooler, and the smell was not so pungent.

"Normally, my Seventeenth Law, Marquis, applies between you and your fellow peers. Not me. I am *not* your peer. Consider yourself fortunate that I find your misinterpretation of my law amusing. So I shall grant you your chance for mediation and the assuagement of grievances," Emperor Xiao said, cybernetically releasing the marquis from his bindings. The minor noble massaged his wrists and gave his back a little twist to relieve the pain caused by standing in that restrained position for so long.

"Your Majesty," the Marquis bowed low, "I believe my actions toward you have been misinterpreted by your earnest intelligence and security forces."

Xiao put a hand on his hip above his own pistol. "Oh? You believe my people laid hands upon a member of my court in error?"

"I am not implying malice, Your Majesty. I'm quite sure Marshal Dynne was acting in the best of faith at your behest." The high judge gave a faint deferential bow toward the lawman.

Marshal Dynne hid his disgust with the scraping and fancy begging.

"Marquis de Yevgenni," Xiao addressed the minor nobleman, "I shall save you the embarrassment of trying to concoct a fable out of whole graphine. I've known what you and your allies have been up to for years now. It shouldn't be a secret, but it is oft forgotten that I know everything that is said by members of my court."

The emperor stepped close to the marquis, "Nothing slips past my eye, very much like your Purgatorian god."

The marquis swallowed hard.

Marshal Dynne's eyes narrowed at the comparison. Purgatorians came from the ancient religion of Christianity, except they believed that the Dream was Purgatory and that the day they died here was when they went to final judgment. A useful tool for keeping their faithful masses in line.

"And much like your faith," the emperor continued, "though most would deny it, I do allow for redemption. Having an effective double agent among the rebellion is always useful for me and imperial security." He turned to smile at Marshal Dynne.

The lawman locked his face into a military-neutral expression, having no idea how to take this casual conversation. It felt like the emperor was bringing him inside some sort of joke, but he could not tell what it was.

The emperor chuckled and gave a hint of a head shake at the marshal's sudden stiffness.

"Redemption, you said?" The marquis repeated, his voice tight and eyes hardening with resolve.

"Oh, yes," Xiao said, looking around at the Silicane forest beneath them. As they went over a small rise, he pointed down into a valley, half shrouded in steam. "There, pilot, just on the edge. Put us down there."

The barge began its gentle descent.

"What sort of redemption would you give?" The marquis asked. "Are you talking about forgiving my political sins against you? Would I remain a high judge?"

"Don't be foolish," the emperor said. "I cannot have a corrupt and disgraced nobleman running my courts or any of my fiefs."

The thought horrified Marshal Dynne.

It seemed the marquis knew it too and pursed his lips with the emperor's sour words. "I see. What good would my service be to you if I was redeemed? You would never trust me enough to put me to good use."

"You assume to know more about my needs and purposes than you ought, Marquis. My ways are mysterious and unknowable. Common sentients like yourself should not try to fathom my desires."

"Assume your... purposes?" The nobleman looked just as confused as Marshal Dynne felt.

The barge set down in the stench again, but now sulfur and other noxious fumes added to the mix. It was a hair's breadth from unbearable. Before them were boiling springs, geysers and bubbling mud pots.

"Redemption in your case will be purchased with a Trial By Ordeal," the emperor said with a broad smile.

"That's barbaric!" The marquis blurted out.

"Is this still law?" Marshal Dynne asked in shock.

"Of course it's law, Marshal. How could you have forgotten? Must we revisit your training and redo your Imperial Qualification Exams?"

"Hail Xiao! No, Your Majesty!" Marshal Dynne shouted, back stiffening in attention.

The emperor's eyebrow rose and fell. "At least you remember your proper conduct."

"What ordeal are you asking me to accomplish?" the marquis demanded.

"Look between the mud pots and boiling springs. Do you see the pile of diamonds? Yes, over there. Sitting on that small rise of rocks next to the steaming geyser."

Marshal Dynne followed the emperor's finger which pointed to a glittering stack of cut diamonds in a clear foam of epoxy.

"Yes?" the Marquis de Yevgenni said. His mouth developed a mild twitch.

Marshal Dynne started making connections on what was about to happen as well.

"Bring it back to me and you shall be redeemed in my eyes and granted mercy. No matter the result, my ways are served. This is your ordeal."

Dynne could see that the former high judge knew there was a catch not being included. The heat, steam and splashing of the geothermal hazards were hard to ignore.

"May I have something to carry your prize in?"

"Be resourceful," the emperor said tartly.

"What about the monsters? Will you keep them back?" the marquis asked.

"No, but here." The emperor drew his own blaster, pulled out the magazine to reveal a full charge, and put it back in.

"Your Majesty!" Marshal Dynne protested as the emperor tossed the pistol underhanded to the marquis. As the firearm hung in the air, the lawman could figuratively see the calculations going through the traitorous marquis' head. Dynne's hand went for his own sidearm.

The Marquis de Yevgenni caught the pistol and locked eyes on the electric blue gaze of the emperor. Everyone froze. The eyes of the Glassmen became pairs of painfully bright sodium orange light, locked on the high judge. The Janus-faced guards were ready to fire.

"If you think your forfeit is worth the risk, Marquis, I suggest you take it," Xiao's voice was so low it was barely audible over the plopping and splashing of the nearby mud pots. A geyser gave off a loud hiss.

"Certain death for the chance to kill you? A trade of my life for yours?" the marquis asked.

"But what does it matter to a Purgatorian like yourself? You die, you are free of Purgatory and on to what you believe is your salvation," Emperor Xiao tempted, showing more of his chest.

"It's suicide. That would mean damnation," the marquis said.

"No, it's an exchange. You might survive. Killing me may stay my servant's hands. That means it's not suicide. Unless you wish to *consider* it murder, but we both know that in your heart, you don't," the emperor summarized.

"I know what a rigged gambit looks like and choose to lean on the old proverb that discretion is the better part of valor," the marquis returned.

"Is that from your religious tracts?" Xiao asked coyly.

Marshal Dynne breathed a sigh and took his hand off the grip of his sidearm.

"Just an old homily. It surprises me you didn't know that, for someone vaunted to be omniscient. No, I suspect that you have rigged this trial by ordeal too, but I am still more likely to survive."

"Maybe you can use it as a test of faith too?" Xiao taunted. "If the ordeal is rigged, perhaps your god is more powerful than an actual divine being in the flesh?"

"Apostasy and abomination," the marquis mumbled his face a mask of disgust.

"Then be about it. Show me your worth. Succeed and gain a reward beyond mere forgiveness of your sins against me," Xiao said with a huff.

The marquis looked down the winding path between him and the pile of diamonds, planning his route carefully. Like spectators watching their team rally in an attempt to win a come-from-behind victory, the emperor and Marshal Dynne focused on the prisoner.

The goal was not even a hundred yards away, but he would have to zigzag through mud pots and boiling water splashing from geysers along his path. The marquis' foot made a delicate crunching sound as the spongy surface gave a little beneath his weight. Thin crystalline deposits crackled and spread out like thin ice, but held his weight. The noble looked back at his emperor with a bitter scowl.

Xiao smiled. "Not rigged, but absolutely more challenging than you anticipated."

In the distance of the vegetation, alien eyes intently watched the marquis take measured steps. He tested the ground as he moved giving him a strange dance-step pace that moved him safely between patches of firm footing. He began to hiss in pain for his shoes did not protect him from the heat radiating through the ground. One of the crystals he hopped onto gave way beneath him, squirting up a sulfurous fume of boiling water that splashed him with blistering droplets, but he did not fall through.

Xiao the Eternal gave a laugh of surprised amusement.

Marshal Dynne looked on in horror. Yes, the man was a traitor. Yes, he deserved to die, and even to suffer torture, but that was at the hands of the law! This? This was just luck and happenstance. There was no justice here. Just sick amusement. What if he succeeded? Where is the merit? How could Xiao use such a man?

A shriek tore out of the marquis as a thick gout of mud-spattered him, burning his flesh even through prison clothing. He dropped the pistol as several fingers on his right hand blistered up. Reaching down, he gathered the gun up into his left hand and ran on. The cooked muscle of his leg made him limp toward the small rise where his goal sat in the boiling runoff of a hot spring.

Sheets of water pulsed and rushed over the bright yellow rock, wetting the base of the diamond-filled stack. The marquis looked around for a way to get closer. Using the Emperor's pistol, he blasted off a large chunk of a mushroom tree and threw the fat lightweight crescent into the scalding water to act like a stepping stone. Then he threw out three more creating a path.

As he readied to cross the scorching liquid, several creatures crawled out from the disturbed fungus towards him. They were silicone parodies of animals. Small floating jellies floated down from the damaged tree, their tendrils reaching out, dripping with some sort of fluid that hissed and smoked on the ground beneath them. The marquis opened fire. P-beams crackled, killing the closest monsters to him, and the creatures retreated. A corpse was dragged away to be eaten by its comrades.

Marshal Dynne was shocked to discover he felt the smallest hope for the former high judge. The man was fighting with all his being to be worthy. Out of the corner of his eye, he saw a contemptible smirk on the emperor's face. Was he enjoying the suffering?

With a careful twist, the marquis removed his shirt. Marshal Dynne's skin crawled as he saw the blisters and red patches on the marquis' pale flesh. The mushroom tree chunks rocked and wobbled as he walked out toward the stack. With a wrapped hand, he tried to tug the pile free. It was stuck. He gave it another jerk and the stack bent and contorted, but did not give.

There came a sharp, crackling buzz in the Silicane forest. It was near, but not visible, and it was big.

A splash of burning steam wafted over the marquis who squealed in pain. He looped his shirt around the stack again and gave a hard pull. The stack tore free and sent him sprawling with his prize into the scalding water. He shrieked and scrambled out of the water, his screams turning into low grunts with the effort.

Carefully, clutching the hot epoxied stack of diamonds to his cheek, he ran as best he could on his cooked legs. Marshal Dynne was wracked with sympathetic pain as the marquis' feet kept busting through the thin crust of ground and were burned even more. Dimly, he hoped the man's pain receptors were utterly dead for he was running on the meat that remained.

Marshal Dynne realized he'd been holding his breath. Softly, he forced himself to start again so the emperor did not hear. A look of joy filled the marquis' face as he closed in on the barge, only a few dozen feet to go.

This time, the crackling buzzing roar was deafening.

Out of the vegetation burst a creature that Marshal Dynne could never have conceived in his nightmares. There was no time for the marquis to scream for the monstrosity slammed into the man, mouth first, at terrific speed. The pistol and the stack of epoxied diamonds flew toward the barge. Marshal Dynne stared in horror as the thing chewed the marquis' body up with a ravenous purpose.

It was twelve feet in diameter, looking like an angler fish and lionfish spliced together with a rocket propelled dirigible. The slimy skin was translucent and reflective gray on top with glittering hard diamonds for its underbelly. Two lobster-like claws protruded from either side. Its mouth looked like a catcher's mitt filled with molars and incisors when it flared open.

With a self-satisfied hum, Emperor Xiao stepped off the barge. Ignoring the grisly sight happening not a few feet away from him, the monarch scooped up his pistol and then his prize. Before stepping back onto the barge, he regarded the creature with amused disdain.

As the barge rose pulled away he spoke, "Mycoliths are voracious and very protective of their egg broods." Xiao's tone was positively chilly in its clinical nature.

"Maybe his soul will be collected unto his god now. His body served me well in his last act. Though if he really believed that silly superstition, he would have tried to kill me. The trade wouldn't have been worth it, but he would have died believing he did the right thing."

"Why would that concern you, Your Majesty?"

"Hope makes the revelation of true failure all the more painful. Build someone up for the purpose of watching them fall, and the end result can be spectacularly amusing."

Marshal Dynne felt a cold warning deep in his soul.

"Hail Xiao," he said softly with a conspiratorial smile he did not feel.

The Eternal Emperor, the All-Seeing Eye looked at his marshal and smiled in return.

"Let's go back to court and have some dinner while we speak of your future, Marshal Dynne."

#   #   #

THE WAKING NIGHTMARES

PREVIEW

Warm light poured down over Winston as Puala'Lolo's rotation took him out of the faint shade of the palm tree. He snored contentedly in a lounge chair in the early afternoon till the baking sand's heat gently woke him up.

He looked off into the seemingly endless distance to the ocean's edge. Bright white local clouds puffed up into little thunderheads like ancient sailing ships, while above them the grandiose clouds of the Dream drifted by in pale pastel pinks, teals and oranges common to its tropical upper layers.

Life here had been a veritable spa as part of his convalescence following their departure from Nova Tortuga. The last few weeks out of the cab at this height of the Dream turned his skin tan.

He picked up his "Plammer" and took a swig. The ice cold sweat felt good in his hand, and the mix of iced tea and lemonade was perfect for his lazy mood.

At some point, he realized that this was his first vacation ever, even if it was due to a cavalcade of suffering. A bitter bubble of memory rose to the surface as he realized he could not share this moment with Val and Emmy. An ice cold drop of water hit his chest and popped the recollection, and he sighed at its passing.

Reaching over to the little table, Winston picked up his pocket assistant and checked the time, and put it back. He'd been sleeping peacefully for over two hours.

Maybe it was the aftereffects of the brainburn, or all the neuro therapy he had been undergoing with Doctor Amanda Junker, but even his nightmares refused to come to this paradise.

In the surf, Billy Joe Bob was fishing, using his own transmogrified utility sand arms as rod, reel, line and lure. He had generated a creel in his utility skirt. Winston never considered a mechoid being interested in fishing, but there he was, fishing away.

The waves washed around his nanosand skirt as if he was a tide rock. At least he wasn't noodling, Winston thought with a faint smile. Then again, this sort of behavior could blame it on that personality mod he'd been using.

Since setting foot on Puala'Lolo neither one dared to use the Sierra Madre's mainframe even to access idle entertainments. Thanks to the battle between Mother and the Bonavitae hacker, it was riddled with viruses and other dangerous programs that could snatch Billy Joe's consciousness out of his CPU, just as easily as it could scramble Winston's frontal lobe. Besides, they had permissions now for the local network, but neither had felt the need to log in.

Bubby landed another fish. It was a big, exotic thing. Possibly a ray of some type, flapping its huge wings in frantic splashes of water as he hauled it to the surface.

"Check it out, Hoss!" Bubby shouted back to Winston. "Hoo-boy! Look at it!"

Winston saluted him, raising his drink high.

Like a cheerful kid getting approval from his parents, Billy Joe held up his catch high. "Take a picture!"

"Why? You can replay that memory later."

"Come on! I want it from your point of view!" he shouted as he wrestled to hold on to the fish that was almost half his size and fighting. His drive skirt spread out in a lattice of columns to help keep balance, his arms wrapped around the fish to hold on a few more seconds.

Winston reached over, picked up his pocket assistant, and snapped the picture. Billy Joe smiled and reabsorbed his fishing gear into his arm and tossed the critter out into the water with a flat smack. The ray took off like a shot.

Billy Joe slid up out of the surf and over to Winston, smiling from ear to ear. "It's no industrial press video, but I have found something soothing about this sport."

"To Bubby, the mechoid fishing champeen of the Dream. Who'da thunk?"

Billy Joe gave a goofy, auto-tuned musical laugh.

Down the beach came a hovercar. It was an exotic touristy sort of thing with open sides and a fabric canopy that fluttered with a fringe.

"Oops. Looks like playtime's over," he said, giving a head jut up the dunes toward the Baron's compound. One of the Baroness's personal guard came to collect them.

With a groan, Winston slung his feet off the lounge chair and readied to stand.

"I'm not looking forward to this either, Hoss, but what else can we do?" Billy Joe said. Winston's own sadness echoed in his partner's voice.

"Like watching your favorite horse getting put down in her prime," Winston agreed. With a few big swallows, he polished off his drink, put it on the small table, and stood up.

"Mechsters Winston and Billy Joe?" the driver
addressed the pair as they walked to the
hovercar.

"Yah, yah. Keep yer pants on," Winston said,
putting on his straw panama hat and sandals that
completed his beach bum appearance. The two
climbed aboard and were off. The hovercar
glided over the dunes and deeper into the island
compound grounds.

#　　#　　#

End of Preview

THANKS & ACKNOWLEDGMENTS

I would like to acknowledge the contributions of the following people:

Editor
Jane Lambert

Alpha Readers
Ben & Shannon Stepanek

Special 'thank yous' to:

Bridget Boncher

Wordmenders Critique Group: Stephanie Dooley, K.T. Sweet, Nathan Veyon, Jenn Lees, & Phillip Wilder.

Thank you all!

Dear Reader, if you enjoyed this story, please leave a review where you purchased your copy! Let people know what you think. If you write a review or vlog, send us the link so we can boost your reach. Media and others interested in interviews, contact us at www.resonantmedia.art . Thank you!

MDB